BOOK THREE OF THE VAMPIRE WAR

NIGHT FALL

CHRONICLES OF THE OTHERWORLD

MELISSA CUMMINS

Published by Melissa Cummins on January 17th, 2023

ISBN: 978-1-958769-00-3, 9781958769027

ALSO BY MELISSA CUMMINS

CHRONICLES OF THE OTHERWORLD

Part 1. The Vampire War

Dark Vampire and Witch Romance (Interconnected Standalones best read in this order)

Night Shade

Night Fury

Night Fall

Part 2. Feral Wolves - Coming Soon

Dark Omegaverse/Shifter Romance (Standalones read in any order)

Carnal Claim - Coming Soon

Bitten To Obey - Coming Soon

Primal Hunger - Coming Soon

Savage Embrace - Coming Soon

Part 3. Fae - Coming Soon

Dark Fae Romance (Standalones best read in any order)

Fae Book 1 - Coming Soon

Fae Book 2 - Coming Soon

Fae Book 3 - Coming Soon

STANDALONES

My Brutal Beast

Crowned In Blood

My Vicious Beast - Coming Soon

DEDICATION

To those who like their men commanding, morally gray, and willing to kill and burn the bodies of anyone who would even dare breathe the same air as them. And to the women who are just as violent and unpredictable. Stay stabby my friends.

NEVER MISS A RELEASE

To get information on works in progress, new releases, and receive exclusive discounts, giveaways, and bonus content, make sure to subscribe to my newsletter!

AUTHOR'S NOTE

Night Fall took me on an incredible journey. This book has changed my life. The character's stories have entranced and inspired me, and I hope they do the same for you.

This book is dark, as you'll see from some of the triggers below. I am always wary of calling a book dark as everyone has their own definition of what that entails. This book deeply explores grief, death, suicide, rape, injustice, slaughter, wars, disease, and some of the darker times of history. There may be times you might not like the characters, or times you may feel their morals have gone out of the window. There may be times their behavior and the choices they make shock you. Don't worry, you're supposed to feel that way.

This isn't just a tale of romance, smut, kinks, or your typical protective and possessive alpha hero. While yes, Night Fall does have all of those things, this book is about finding yourself, and the journey you sometimes have to take to heal the parts of you that you didn't even know existed. It's about letting someone see the sides of you that you think are weak, and finding someone who will show you that you're strong. It's about learning to lean on someone, to let them in.

Night Fall is the third in the Chronicles of The Otherworld series, as well as the third book in part one,

The Vampire War. Each part of the series will feature a different paranormal species. Each book will feature a different couple and will always have a Happy Ever After (HEA) for that couple.

The tropes are: Taboo (Guardian/Charge), Age Gap, Fated Mates, Second Chance, First Love, Virgin, Billionaire Hacker/Assassin heroine, Protective, possessive, billionaire anti-hero, Kidnapped and tortured, Betrayal, Morally gray couple, Touch her/him and die vibes, Return From The Dead, Found Family, and Coming of Age.

While I always recommend reading from beginning of the series for the best experience, Night Fall is an interconnected standalone.

Night Fall is intended for mature audiences. This story contains mentions and detailed depictions of physical, emotional, mental, and sexual abuse, including rape and sexual harassment, suicidal thoughts and attempts, extreme violence, murder, death, torture, explicit language, sexually explicit scenes, and blood drinking.

This book also discusses and depicts grief, deaths of love ones, near death experiences, war, negative self-talk, feelings of unworthiness and inadequacy, criticism, depression, and amnesia.

The following kinks have also been included in this work: begging, praise, degradation, Pleasure Dom and Brat behavior, breath play, and spanking.

Reader discretion is advised.

PLAYLIST

Want to listen along while you read? Search CoTO: Night Fall on Spotify or scan the QR code below:

Iris - The Goo Goo Dolls

Can't Help Falling In Love - DARK - Tommee Profitt, Brooke

War of Hearts - Ruelle

Good Enough - Evanescence

Hurts Like Hell - Fleurie, Tommee Profitt

Still Here - Digital Daggers

Falling Apart - Skylar Grey

Dancing With Your Ghost - Sasha Alex Sloan

First Thing To Go - Hayley Williams

Razors Edge - Digital Daggers

Letters From The Sky - Civil Twilight

Far Away - Nickelback

Heal Over - KT Tunstall

Inside Out - Zedd feat. Griff
Royalty - Egzod, Maestro Chives, Neoni
Never Stop (Wedding Version) - SafetySuit
Queen Of The Night - Hey Violet

PROLOGUE

The first time she met him, she was dying.

The plague had taken over villages, entire conti-
nents. So many lives had been lost and now that tally
included her mother, father, and aunt. Mya tried to take
care of them, tried to hope that if she could just do
something, that if she was fast enough, worked hard
enough, they would survive. And if not, at least she
could help them hold on until her brother, Gregori,
came back with a cure. He would come back; she was
sure of it. They all just had to stay strong and have faith
until then.

But hours turned into days, days into weeks, and
still Gregori was gone. And now she, and her cousin,
Lucas, had fallen ill.

Waiting for a cure changed to waiting for death. Mya
could feel the Black Plague eating away at her flesh,
fogging her mind, ruining her, turning her into some-

thing other than the young, healthy, vibrant girl she once was.

At the end, there was no one left to watch over them. No one to feed them, wash them, or ease their suffering. Mya and Lucas had tried so hard not to succumb to the illness, but eventually they collapsed on the floor, and soon they were covered in their own boils, piss, vomit, and fecal matter, too weak to move. If the plague did not kill them, starvation would.

It was difficult to know she was dying and could not do a single thing about it. Mya did not want to die, but what was the alternative? Even if Gregori came back with a cure, it would never revive the limbs she lost to gangrene, or the delirium that had set in at her high fever. And who was to say that Gregori was still alive? He may be just as dead as she was bound to be.

That was the state Gregori had found them in. She could not see clearly by the time Gregori and his companion entered their small family home. She half thought she had imagined his return. But then she heard his companion's voice, and it stole her entire focus. Mya did not know what it was about that voice. She had heard men speak before, and while she and Lucas had been alone for some time, she still remembered the voices of the other inhabitants of their village ... back when they were still alive, that was. Still, the slightly accented voice—so deep and rich, patient and controlled, yet strained, as if he cared about her survival —touched her, deeply. That there was anyone left to care when she was so close to death warmed her heart, made her suffering ease just slightly.

It was a mixture of that feeling and the panic in Gregori's voice that made tears spill from her eyes. It was too late. She was too far gone, and she wished her brother had been saved from seeing her like this so that he could remember her the way she was before the plague, before he left. Yet her single string of happiness came from the notion that he would be by her side when she died.

Her wish to have him near her was a selfish one. She looked up to him, respected him, wanted more for him, but also needed him. He gave her the courage she needed to accept her death without bitterness or resentment.

But then she felt his presence next to her. He was far too close. And what about Lucas? Why was Gregori not going to Lucas? Had he already died? Was she the only one left, deliriously waiting for hope when there was none?

No, there may not be hope for her, and perhaps there was no hope for her cousin, but Gregori should survive. He *needed* to survive, which meant he needed to leave this plague infested house and save himself.

Gregori moved to cradle her, but she pushed him away. He leaned over her once more, and she fought with all her might to shove him once again. That bought her a few inches, but she was too weak for anything more.

Gregori warned her not to fight him, but still she thrashed. She sobbed in their native tongue, warning him, *begging* him to save Lucas, and if he could not, to at least save himself.

Then a hand, heavy but gentle, grasped her shoulder, surging warmth through her body. Mya's blurry eyes shifted to Gregori's companion's as the man spoke for the first time, "Be still. Gregori has brought you a cure. Listen to your brother and take it."

The last of her energy fled from her as if it had been washed away by a great tide, and she fell back onto the hard floor, so tired that she could do nothing more but obey. The stranger touched her again, his hand shifting to her jaw where he squeezed until he forced her to open her cracked and bleeding lips.

Liquid dripped into her mouth and slid to the back of her throat. She swallowed, and the first wave of heat hit her, pleasurable and shocking. Mya could suddenly taste a fury of flavors—acidic, meaty, savory, salty, iron, and something almost close to smoke. Every part of her being came alive as fire burst through her body, setting her aflame. She felt renewed, energized, capable, stronger than she had ever been in her entire life. She wanted more of the delicious drink; she *craved* it.

Unable to control her fervor and now free from the stranger's touch, she grasped her brother's hand to her lips and sunk her teeth—no, no longer teeth ... *fangs*—into Gregori's wrist, drinking his blood in mouthfuls. She should have been disgusted by the notion, concerned by her illness, but she was too lost to the power he had given her through his blood. It was only when the stranger pulled her away, did she settle calmly onto her back, high on something she could not name.

She felt her brother leave her and move to the side where she had last seen her cousin. After several moments, her eyes focused and she glanced at the unknown being in front of her. A gasp left her lips at his beauty, and she blushed at the twitch of a smile on his lips, embarrassed by her state of undress and filth.

That was the first time she met Erik Devereux, and he looked like an angel.

CHAPTER 1

Mya hated England. She hated its up-and-coming center, preferring the old, rocky, dirt roads of Spain. She missed playing on them, getting her feet dirty, her clothing soiled. She missed the simplicity of it all. There was something natural about the Spanish landscape, something England could not grasp no matter how many times it attempted to with its perfectly spaced, manicured trees. It was not wild, not like her. But England was her home now.

Erik had become her family's guardian. Due to his status as lord of the region, Erik was able to keep Gregori out of England's upcoming wars. He took on the task of tutoring both Gregori and Lucas in a variety of subjects, from education to creative skills, and, lastly, battle.

He had hired a female tutor for Mya, hoping to give her someone to relate to. But that was an impossible task. Mya did not care for the woman and only agreed to attend her lessons so she could play outside afterward. That was the only time she felt free. She climbed the tall oak trees, chased insects, and tore through the garden beds on her adventures to "help" their chef. She would flee to the stables, sneaking around the stablemen to slip fruit and vegetables to the horses, but it was that last forbidden adventure that had her crying on the back stairs that afternoon.

She heard the crunching of rock under boots in front of her. Then she heard them pause. She knew by the sound of the steps that it was Erik, but she refused to meet his gaze. She did not want him to see her cry. He did so much for them, for her. He spoiled her and she knew he gave her far too much attention. Even unhappy, Mya did not want to seem ungrateful or make things harder on Erik or her family. But Erik knew her intrinsically. She did not know how, but he knew what she needed, and no matter how determined she was to handle her issues on her own, Erik would not let her. And he always got his way.

Erik slipped his hands under her arms, lifting her. Then he turned and took her place on the seat, setting her in his lap, a habit he had continued from when she was a child. He held her with her back to his chest and let her sit there in silence as more tears rolled down her cheeks, turning into full sobs of sorrow.

When she quieted, Erik asked, "Why are you crying, *fagr skjaldmær min?*"

Mya shook her head. "I am not crying."

He laughed, the sound as comforting as the warm rays of the sun. "Then what is the reason for the waterfalls pouring from your eyes?"

She shook her head with a small grunt.

Erik ran his fingers through her long dark tresses, bunching the curled strands between his fingers. "Tell me, *fagr skjaldmær min.*"

"When will you tell me what that means?" Mya asked, attempting to distract him as she sniffled and leaned more into his body, letting his strength run through her.

"When you are older."

When she pouted, and turned her head to face him, he said. "Now, Mya."

She sighed. "One of the stablemen..." She paused, glancing at Erik to see how much trouble she would be in for wandering around the horses.

"I already know where you go, *fagr skjaldmær min.*"

She gasped. "You do?"

"Of course I do. Why do you think I hired extra men? Their job is to watch over you, if I am otherwise engaged, and ensure none of the horses hurt you." Erik dropped a soft kiss to her temple. "There are not many places you could go that would escape my gaze. It is my job, my *duty*, to be there for you should you ever need me, and it is a role I take very seriously."

Mya blushed, but she did not know why. She was not sure what to call the level of affection and admiration that spiraled through her heart at his words. He made her feel safe, she realized, a feeling she had only felt before with her parents. Then the crawling feeling of misery tugged sharply at her heart once more and she had to stop herself from crying again.

"One of the stablemen asked if I was your daughter," she finally said. "I-I know he did not mean any harm, but it made me think about Papa and Mama." She trembled, and Erik drew her closer as if he wished to physically banish her grief. "I try not to think about them too often. It hurts so much when I do. I was not strong enough to protect them." She shook her head. "I should have been stronger."

"Mya–"

"What if it happens again?" she hiccupped.

Erik wiped the tears from her eyes. "We are vampires now. We do not have to worry about the plague—"

"But there are other things. You are always training Gregori and Lucas to fight because humans can kill us, yet you will not train me. Is it because I am too weak? Is it because you can only see me as a girl? Do you see me as nothing but a young woman, a child, too young to be useful? Your pseudo-daughter—"

"No," Erik said so sternly that it felt as if the world stopped. "You are not weak." He paused and stroked the soft skin of her cheek. "I remember the day Gregori brought me to you. I remember how hard you tried to fight to save Gregori from contracting the disease. Those are not the actions of a weakling. And I could never see you as a child, nor as my daughter."

Mya was too stunned to say anything, and he took advantage of her silence. "I see you as something so much more. Something more beautiful, more *fantastical* than I could ever explain to you. I cannot see you as I see Gregori and Lucas, nor can I treat you the same way I treat them. You hold my heart in a way that no one else ever will, and that love allows me to see you, to see through you into this thing here." He lightly poked at her chest, right above her heart. "You are strong, *fagr skjaldmær min*, and I am honored to be able to witness that strength every day."

She shattered, tossing her arms around Erik's neck hugging him as she cried into his body. His long, pale blonde hair tickled her face, neck, and shoulder as she stole into his warmth. He held her, gently rocking with her and rubbing her back until the grief of her parents' death left her.

The silence brought back his words, and Mya tried to analyze her own feelings for the man who had helped save her life. There was so much to Erik that she treasured, and yet so much she did not understand, including her feelings for him.

He was everywhere and everything to her. He was there when the memory of her near death kept her awake at night. He tucked her in and waited until she was asleep before he left. He was there to speak with her, to carry her, play with her, read to her. He fed her, clothed her, listened to her words, her thoughts. He valued her. Without him she would have nothing, she would *be* nothing.

But it was more than that.

She respected the man she found herself watching far too often. She respected how he treated those around him. He was stern but just, a merciful enforcer who both defended his lands and inspired his people. He was intelligent, courageous, brave. He gave so much and asked for so little back. To Mya, he was a symbol of perfection—something she should not be able to reach—that blessed her each day and night.

But what did all of that mean? She loved Erik in a way she did not love her brother or cousin. Mya did not have any companions, but she knew what she felt for Erik was more than that. If Erik asked her to lay down her life for him, she would do it with a smile.

It was not adoration or pure devotion. It was a simplistic need to bring him whatever level of joy she could, to give him something of what he gave to everyone else: A chance for survival. A chance for happiness. A second chance at life.

So there, in that moment, even though he had not asked and even though she did not have a clear understanding of her feelings, she gave him what she could, something she had not given anyone outside of her family.

"You are in my heart too, Erik." Mya exhaled, and he shivered. "I do not know the love I feel for you. I have not felt it before, but it is there, nonetheless. It is all-consuming and never ending."

Erik's supple lips curled at her temple, then he inhaled as if he could breathe her in. "And for that, I am truly blessed."

———

Mya thought to skip her visit to the stables the following day, not wanting to repeat what happened before, but she pushed through her fear. She enjoyed tending to the horses, and as a strong woman, she refused to be chased away from something that made her happy. So, with her basket of apples, carrots, and celery, Mya held her head high and entered the massive archway.

Every head snapped away from the sight of her, causing her confidence to drop. The stablemen normally did not pay attention to her, but this level of avoidance was unsettling. They seemed to cower with every step she took.

Mya knew that she did not inspire fear, and the only person she knew that did—Erik—was not in the stables. Mya would have known if he was behind her. He always smelled of pine, ash, smoke, and cinnamon, scents that brought her comfort and peace.

Still, she turned to check, but he was nowhere in sight. When she turned back to the men, they were already busying themselves with their normal day to day tasks, ensuring that their backs were to her.

Mya would have thought she had imagined the whole thing if it were not for the way the men scattered away from her every time she passed near them to feed one of the horses. They had never been overly friendly or conversational with her, above and beyond the watchful nature of their roles, but the way they veered away from her now, and the eyes that followed her back when she moved, did not feel like mere curiosity. Instead of apathy, they treated her as if she was a blight that could infect them.

She shrugged. Their actions made no matter to her. In all actuality she preferred to be left alone; speaking to people took too much energy from her, and she found their conversations not only tiring but uninspiring. Still, the sudden change was strange, but that was not the only thing that struck her as odd.

Mya had kept an eye out for the stableman who had spoken to her the day before, desperate to not run into him again, but as the morning wore on, she realized that she had not seen him at any of the usual posts in the stables or out on the field.

When Erik came to tuck her in later that night, she decided to give voice to the thoughts in her head.

"I went to the stables today," she said, studying him.

His entire body seemed to still, except for one small tic in his hand as he gripped the top of her comforter. His silver eyes met her own, and she noticed how hard they were. "I know. How were the horses?"

"Well, but—"

"Then I am overjoyed to hear you enjoyed your time."

His tone was clipped, angry, and it confused her as he turned to walk away. Mya nearly let him, but she could not stop the words that tumbled from her mouth.

"Did you do something to that stableman?"

Again, Erik froze. His fists balled, clenched, then extended. She could see the tension in each movement, yet he did not answer her.

"Erik, did you do—"

"No one hurts you, Mya."

Her mouth dropped open, then closed quickly. She sat up, holding the comforter to her chest. "But he did not hurt me. It was my fault."

A rush of air hit her face as Erik appeared in front her, his nose mere centimeters from hers. His eyes were controlled, cold, *dangerous*, and it made something in her want something she could not name.

When he spoke, his voice was low, hoarse, drowning in some sort of emotion that made her heart pound and goosebumps snake up her skin.

"He did hurt you. Whether he meant to or not makes no difference to me. That is *inexcusable*," Erik hissed. "He dared to speak to you when he should not have, and by doing so he hurt you. No one hurts what is min—"

Erik took a deep breath and closed his eyes, attempting to settle his anger. His body shuddered as if he was forcing himself back from an invisible ledge.

With another breath he centered himself, peered into her eyes, and said in a deep, controlled tone, "No one hurts what falls under my care."

"The men are not allowed to speak to me?" Mya whispered.

"Correct. They may not speak to you, touch you, or pay attention to you unless completely necessary."

She bit her lip and forced herself to swallow. His control should have felt restrictive. She should have been angry with him, she should have told him she could take care of herself, but instead she felt her skin growing warm as a thrumming began between her thighs and her core grew damp. For a single moment Mya worried she may have gotten her cycle early, but this was not that. This feeling was pleasant, needy, something else that she had never felt before.

Erik's eyes grew darker, the black pupils bleeding over into his normal silver and making them appear gray at the edges. He inhaled as if he were smelling something, tasting the air. His breath grew labored, and a small part of his fang extended beyond his lips.

"Are you not mad at me?" he asked, his voice deeper than she had ever heard it.

Mya shook her head.

"Tell me why," he murmured as he leaned closer to her body, nearly eliminating the distance. He grabbed hold of her hair, twirling it between his fingers while his eyes roamed over her face, drinking in her every expression.

She bit her lip again, her eyes flickering away from his and falling back to his red lips. "I ... appreciate your protection, I suppose."

He hummed, then nodded. "Then I will tell you what I did to the stableman. I stalked him until he was running scared for his life. Then I tore off his head, drained his body of most of its blood, and fed his useless corpse to the pigs. His family will receive a large dowry for his reported accidental death, and none will be the wiser."

She gasped in shock, but the horror she should have felt was missing. Instead, a thrill of pleasure flew through her at how far Erik would go for her. His violence, his protection, made her feel treasured, cherished, reveled in.

"Tell me, Mya, does it scare you that I can be so callous? So cold and brutal?" he taunted.

Her heart felt as though it was going to pound out of her chest, and she grabbed onto his arm for support. His skin was warmer than usual, muscles bunched as he fisted her hair, drawing her head back slightly until she was staring straight into his eyes again. She answered him breathlessly, honestly.

"No."

"Why?" he crooned, and it was as if he was dragging the answer out of her, tearing it from the very depths of her soul.

She licked her suddenly dry lips, wrestling with the emotions he laid bare within her. Mya swallowed, paused, and on a shaky breath said, "Because I know you. I have watched you. I see you for who you are, and I love you and all that you are."

His fingers danced along her scalp sending tingles down her spine, and she whispered, "I am safe with you."

He smiled, his fangs fully protruding now. "Yes, you are, *fagr skjaldmær min.*"

With that Erik inhaled once more and clenched his jaw. Then he stood, and with each step he tugged something open in her, something raw and vicious. Then he paused, his hand on the doorknob, and without turning he said, "Should you face another issue with anyone, the staff, a stranger—"

"I will tell you," she said.

He nodded stiffly as he stood on the threshold. "Goodnight, Mya."

"Thank you," she whispered.

His answer was a curt nod before he left her room.

CHAPTER 2

As the years passed, Mya's body had begun to change and mature. Her breasts grew heavier, fuller, and attracted more attention than she was used to from the town boys, ones who believed themselves to be men worthy of her affections.

According to many, her backside was just as distracting, and she was solely to blame for the males who drooled over her like a piece of meat every time she simply left the house to run an errand. It was her fault for being curvier, womanly, and not procuring clothing to defer their gaze. Some even snickered behind her back that she craved the attention. Ah, yes, because it was Mya's fault they could not stop themselves from staring at her. How she wished she could dig their eyeballs out of their heads—then they would really have something to blame her for.

To them, her silent indifference was her weakness, her admission of guilt. Their gossip soon turned cruel and painful, using her earth-toned skin to question her heritage, to spin the tale that she was a servant's child, that she only claimed to be related to Gregori and Lucas and was not actually their kin. But the worst rumor of all was that she had set her sights on Erik to keep his money for herself.

After all, Mya was eighteen now. According to the villagers she was much too old to still be unmarried. There had to be a reason she had waited so long, especially with her child-bearing hips. How it sounded like they wished her to be nothing more than a cow for a man to breed.

But Mya knew that even without her appearance, she still would have been pursued by mothers and sons alike, just as her family was. She was connected to Erik, lord of the land. Who would not want to court and marry her? She could have any man she wanted at the drop of the hat, except the actual man she wanted, it seemed.

It had gone so far, that Gregori and Lucas had offered to escort her on her adventures into town, all to curb the horrible behaviors Mya was subjugated to, but she refused them both. Their supervision would have made it all the more real, hurtful, and embarrassing.

She hated it all.

Mya hated how men ruled the world. Her parents had always taught her that there were things a man could do and things only a woman could do, but that both were in equal power. Her mother and aunt had lived together, taking care of their entire home from cooking and cleaning, to protecting their land from men who wished to steal it, men who believed there was no way women could take care of such a property.

When Mya's father, Henry, decided he wanted to marry her mother, Eleta, he had to fight to win her affection, but not just in the traditional sense. He had to better her mother's life. She did not need him, so Henry had to make Eleta want him. He had to show her that he would never hold her back, only lift her up. He had to make her love him.

To Mya, that was how a courtship worked. That was the example of love she held all relationships to, and none of the men who harassed, belittled, and accused her, who threw their fathers' dowries at her as if it was something for Mya to be impressed by, lived up to those standards.

No, her heart was reserved for Erik, and Mya did everything she could to be closer to him, to spend more time with him.

She left her wild hair long because she liked the way he played with it, twirling the strands around his fingertips as if he was searching for any reason to be close to her. She liked his scent and loved it even more when he came to her bedroom at night so she could drown herself in him before she went to sleep. She loved to watch Erik when he trained Gregori and Lucas, captivated by the way his muscles tensed and tendons squeezed when he threw a punch or kick, how his light blonde hair swayed around his shoulders as he ducked and rolled, parrying his opponents' attacks. She was jealous of the sweat that rolled down his chest when he was done, and she had taken to embracing him whenever they were alone just to claim a piece of him, even if it was just a simple touch. She understood it was foolish, just as she now understood the name for her body's reactions to him—*desire.*

Her attraction to him had grown into something she never knew she could feel. He was the only one she wanted to kiss her, to touch her, to do other things that she heard about from the married women in town. She wanted Erik to pleasure her, and she wanted to learn how to pleasure him, but the reality was it would never be. He was her guardian, and while she still did not understand the breadth of his feelings for her, she knew her thoughts were impure.

Mya respected Erik. She did her best to pretend that was all she felt, but she was tired of pretending. She did not care if it was wrong. She did not want to be pursued by anyone else, to possibly have to fake entertaining a suitor, or to continue to be on high alert every time she left their house just to fit into this time period.

There was something in her gut that told her it would only spell trouble if she continued, but for now that was the game she played as she donned the blue dress that had been carefully embroidered with golden filagree and small gems, coiled her hair and placed it into its typical net, picked her matching headdress and cloak, and went on her way, all while trying not to stomp her feet too hard while she walked.

Her tutor's general scolding flashed through her head, and she had to force herself to straighten her spine, roll her shoulders back, and keep her chin up. Eventually, as the wind blew against her and the sunshine warmed her skin, Mya's mood improved.

It lightened even more as she entered the local apothecary. Mya had taken up the study of medicine and anatomy privately, as she would never have been allowed to practice. The Black Plague still ran rampant among the poor. As a vampire, she did not need the medicine, but Mya wanted to protect those who had no way to receive the necessary medicine. The poor were subjugated to the filth at the hands of the rich, and it made Mya's stomach ill. She knew she could not change the world, and would not be able to save everyone, but she would do all that she could to make a difference.

She was also fascinated by what medicine could do to her blood. Erik had supplied her with a space to practice her experiments, and he often assisted her in her thirst for knowledge by providing her herbs and the latest medical texts he could find. When he could not provide something she wanted, she stole it, and Erik supported her fully.

Mya took her time perusing the shelves before purchasing what she could without raising suspicion: a few herbs which held medicinal properties. She made a mental note of the herbs she would ask Erik to purchase for her, as well as a new rumored text based on the science of anatomy.

She was pleased when she left the apothecary, but the small skip in her step vanished when a door opened behind her and the Bennet twins stepped out, along with Richard Browne and Walter Godfrey. The Bennet twins were children of a noble who believed he and his family controlled the world and everything in it. They were brash. They stole, they lied, they harassed and assaulted women, and they viewed themselves above reproach. Their friends, Richard and Walter, believed the same.

Mya tried to scurry past them but was cut off by Walter. He attempted to grab her, but her vampire abilities made her faster than him. As she veered around one man, the next came from behind her. She turned, avoiding his grasp as well, and spun, but her basket of herbs unbalanced her and she found herself braced against the alley wall.

The breath rushed out of her as Randolph Bennet neared her, his brother, Gilbert, flanked to his side. She began to panic, not for her sake, but for theirs. It was imperative that no one find out she, her family, or Erik were vampires, and that meant Mya had to practice control in this situation. She had to monitor her emotions, not get too angry, too violent. Yet everything about these men told her that they were not going to let her go with a simple scare. They thought themselves to be powerful, but to her they were simply prey, and if they were not careful, she would catch them and eat them like the predator she was.

Mya stood straight against the wall, pressing back against it as much as possible to put space between herself and them. Before they could open their mouths, she said, "I am on my way home. Erik and the rest of my family are waiting for me. Please let me pass."

Richard snickered while Randolph braced his arm above her head. "I am sure they will not miss you for a couple of minutes."

"It will take longer than that to finish with her," Gilbert said with a smirk.

Mya ignored him and stared Randolph straight in his eyes. "Let me go, Randolph. I am not worth the trouble."

The boys behind him laughed, but Randolph's eyes gleamed as if she had said the exact words he needed to hear. "I would be inclined to agree with you, but you have avoided me at every turn, and for that you have to be punished."

"Randolph—"

"Enough, woman!" Randolph yelled, before he reared back and struck her.

The blow he dealt did not bruise her skin nor cause her any pain, but it shocked her. A feeling of injustice rose within her. How could they do this? Why had they done this? What harm had Mya ever caused them, or this world, to be forced to live such a life? Had she not been kind? Had she not kept to herself, done her best to not be a bother, to not bring trouble down upon others? Had she not tried to help others without asking for anything in return? Did she not deserve more?

You deserve more, a voice said to her.

Her voice. Her subconscious.

Pay attention now, it whispered. *Take your retribution.*

She blinked and the world came back into focus. Her face was against the timber panel of the alley while the men pushed and prodded her from behind. It took the four of them to shove her in place, their strength in numbers.

Air began to whip around her legs, and she gasped.

This was going to happen.

They were going to rape her.

Their laughs and hollers filled her ears, and her body turned numb.

What have I done to deserve this? Why is this happening to me?

Hands shoved her legs apart. She knew it, felt her body move, but reality seemed to distort itself. She was there and not there, just as they were there and not there. It was as if she was no longer in her body.

And yet their laughter remained. It grew louder, and their snide remarks followed as they argued about who would be the first to shove themselves inside of her and who would follow next, and after that, and after that.

Their laughter, their cheers as if they had won an honest victory, their *cruelty*, left a stain on her soul.

You are stronger than this, her subconscious growled.

Was she strong? No. She had always been weak. Had that not been why this world had been so barbaric toward her? Was that not why it had taken everything from her? It had taken her family, her way of life. Even something as simple as her studies and passions were unobtainable because she was a woman. And then there was her heart, so far locked away because she could never have the one person she wanted.

But at least she had herself. She had her body, her mind, her soul, and now these men, these insignificant little creatures, were trying to take them from her.

She hated it. She hated England. She hated the rules she had to follow. She hated the women whose words cut her so deeply. She hated the men that treated her as if she was nothing more than an object available to them whenever and however they wanted.

But most of all, perhaps, she hated herself. She hated that nothing would change no matter what she did or how she did it. She hated that as a woman, she would always be expected to sacrifice for someone else.

Mya knew what she was going to do.

She was going to let her anger rule her. She was going to turn into a vampire, a horrible monster to mankind. She was going to kill these men, and her family would be the ones to pay for it. And she hated herself the most because she could not—would not—stop.

Mya deserved more, and she would take her retribution with a smile.

She grasped the wrist of the nearest man and twisted until he screamed so loudly the sound punctured her ear drums. She healed almost instantly from the injury, but the small flinch of pain only strengthened her resolve.

Her eyes glazed over, her blood lust growing stronger and clouding her vision, until she could only feel the pop of his joints and hear the agonizing screams tearing from his body as she broke his bones. She could taste his blood and smell his sweat in the air—salty and sour, tinged with fear.

When the smell of urine flooded her senses, she threw the man away. His head landed with a loud, wet *whack* against the stones. Mya smiled at the sound and the now fresh scent of oozing blood. It sharpened her predatory senses, and while she still could not see the faces of the other men in front of her, she could make out their forms as they processed the shock of the last few seconds.

Then they pushed, hit, and beat her, but she felt no pain. Their blows did nothing but anger her more. They were still invading her space as if they had the right, as if they owned it, owned her, and their feeble attempts to hurt her were accompanied by berating claims that she had asked for this.

Time seemed to slow around her, every action the speed of a tortoise's next step. She parried each of their blows, moving so fast she could predict their next move from the rush of air that tickled the hair on her skin. It felt as if she was moving in the blink of an eye.

Why had she not done this sooner? This feeling, this freedom, was everything to her, and

Mya laughed loudly as she succumbed further. She lifted her arms, ready to push the men, already planning her next move. Maybe she would castrate them, make sure that they could never do this to another woman again. Perhaps she would just kill them outright, their lives payment for the atrocities she was sure they had forced upon other women. They should have never been brought into this world, and she, in her righteousness, would be their judge, jury, and executioner.

The sound of a door opening interrupted her thoughts, and she hissed at the intrusion.

"Aye! What are you boys doing?" a man shouted, before banging something against a metal pot. The sound stung her, so high pitched against her sensitive hearing that it made her head ring.

She looked up and could make out the face of the man, Tubert. He wobbled out of the door, using the frame to support himself on his wooden leg while he brandished the metal pot in an attempt to look intimidating.

Why had he inserted himself into this? Perhaps Tubert had nothing left to lose. Perhaps he wanted to be of importance to someone. Maybe he simply wanted to do something with his life, play at being the hero to raise his value in society. Perhaps he thought that saving her would garner him a reward.

Whatever was going through the man's mind did not matter. No one would get in the way of her justice, not even this man who played at defending her. If he tried to stop her, she would kill him just as surely as she would delight in killing these men. Until she peered down to Tubert's leg and saw Albin, Tubert's seven-year-old son, standing behind his father.

That was what brought Mya back from the edge and curbed her rage. She could never put a child through what she had gone through; she could never rob a child of their parent.

The blood lust cleared from her eyes, allowing her to see. The men's faces in front of her were white, their eyes wide and unblinking. Past them she saw Walter's body—whether dead or just unconscious she did not know—and her stomach turned under the sick satisfaction that sight gave her.

She needed to leave, now, before she succumbed to her blood lust again.

Mya turned and ran. Shouts rang out behind her, but she did not stop. Instead, she ran faster, scared of what she would do, who she would become, and how much she would like it if she turned back. She had put her family in danger, and she fully believed that Gilbert and his group would do everything in their power to use what had just happened to their advantage.

Many people had converted under the power of the church. Erik may be lord of these lands, but the church would be quick to investigate a claim of demonism. One rumor would be enough to qualify the investigation. Any demand for further proof would seem suspicious, and with so many of the townspeople converting, Erik would fall under scrutiny for not reporting her condition himself. There were already those who wanted to challenge his position, and this one action could finally give them the ability to do so.

Mya had caused this. She had brought this trouble into her home.

But what was the alternative?

Should she have stood there and let them rape her? Was that all she was good for? No. This was a situation where the circumstances would never have been in her favor, and her family would understand that. They would support her actions, she knew that deep in her soul, but she did not want them to endure her decisions as well.

If you kill the men who hurt you, they will not have to, the voice within her said.

Unconsciously, her pace slowed until she halted near a wooden wall.

Was that an option? Could that be her only option?

Yes, the voice hissed, begging her.

Mya could kill them. She could wait for them to be

alone and then hunt them down one by one. She could easily find them. Walter's blood was still on her gown, and where he was the others would be sure to follow. She lifted the gown to her nose and inhaled. The blood was so sweet, so delectable, that her heart pounded in her chest.

Mya grasped onto the wall as her blood lust began to take her over once more. Could she do it? Could she take their lives to spare her family the consequences of her actions?

You will only kill those who deserve it. No one else.

It sounded too good to be true, but as she tossed the thought over in her mind, she knew it was the only way. If she killed them, no one else would know. Her family would be safe and she could leave, go somewhere else, perhaps back to Spain. That thought gave her so much warmth, satisfaction, and pleasure, that it sealed her fate.

Mya turned, a smirk tugging her lips. She gave into her blood lust and her vision faded to red. She took one step and pressed her toes to the path, ready to jump, to soar along the roofs of the buildings until she reached her prey. She lowered herself, feeling her energy build, and then—

An arm wrapped around her torso, the heavy weight keeping her still. Before she could even think to struggle, she was pulled back into the shadow of the alley.

The scent of pine, ash, smoke, and cinnamon hit her on her next inhale, and she froze.

Erik.

He cannot see me like this, she thought. *He cannot know.*

But he stood in front of her, plain as day, and his stare was as tangible as the fingers he ran over the torn areas of her gown.

She tried to speak to him, to tell him to leave her, to let her go, but she was not in control. The words came out garbled, incomprehensible, and it only shamed her more.

"Who touched you, *fagr skjaldmær min?*" he asked, his voice low, so calm and deadly that her skin broke out in chills.

Mya could not tell him. Not only because she could not voice the words, but because it pained her too. Erik's presence had always made her feel safe, as if he were her home. She trusted him to always come to her aid, but the thought of him doing so now threw her into a panic. If she told him, he would take on her battle. He would kill the men she was meant to kill, and therein lay the problem.

This was not for him to solve. This was not for him to do. She could not rely on him this time, and she refused to let him interfere. Too much could go wrong, and she would not let him implicate himself in his act of heroism. She wanted to prove to herself, to him, that she was just as much as a warrior as he, that she could be just as ruthless, calculating, and brave.

She would not miss this chance.

She would not let those men win.

Her blood lust pulsed under her emotions, twisting her desires into a desperate need for survival. The weight of her embarrassment, shame, guilt, anger, disappointment, hatred, and love merged into something ugly, and for the first time in her life she fought against Erik. She tried to push him away. When that did not work, she tried to hit and punch him, but he simply grabbed her hands by her wrists and shoved her back against the wall. The movement only made her fight more. Her consciousness ached because she could not break out of her blood lust.

She felt outside of her body again, and the sight she saw devastated her. She did not recognize the woman struggling against Erik. She was so lost, so chaotic, her jaw snapping at him as she tried to free her hands and claw at his skin. Mya would have never tried to hurt Erik. She did not want to rely on him, and she wanted him to let her go, but not like this. This was not her, but she did not know how to regain her senses.

Tears dropped from her lashes as she realized that even with this power, she was weak. If she could not use her mind and be in control of her heart and body, what good was she to anyone?

She tried again to speak to Erik. The words were even more garbled now, coming out as feral, animalistic sounds and snarls, but somehow he knew. Erik used his body to keep her pinned against the wall. He grabbed hold of her neck, grasping it between his thumb and pointer finger. His hands were so large that his fingers reached under her ear, but his touch was gentle as he whispered, "I will not let you suffer this, *fagr skjaldmær min*. Forgive me."

His free hand slid into her hair, fisting the strands at her scalp. He tilted her face to his, holding her in place and then his lips came down against hers.

CHAPTER 3

Everything in her stopped.

Her fight, her thoughts, her heart, her very breath all ground to a halt when he kissed her.

Sensations she had never known took her over. Erik's lips were soft, so warm and firm against her own. Gently he moved them against hers, and eventually she began to follow his movements. Mya did not feel the shift in her blood lust, did not even sense that it had started to die down, that the emotions that had once powered her change were now morphing into something else, something undeniable, incontrollable: *desire.*

Erik broke away from her, leaving her gasping both for breath and for his return. Mya tried to follow, but his hand was still in her hair, grasping the strands tighter, and she hoped, nearly prayed, that it meant he felt a shred of what she did.

Mya wished she could voice the words, that she was

more experienced in this, but she was too breathless, too shocked and senseless to be able to speak. Then she peered into his silver eyes, and she saw it: the same desire was mirrored in them, an abundant hunger that was both dark and heavenly.

One moment, just one breath, passed, as if he was trying to win some internal battle, and then he was back on her again. She welcomed him. She knew better now, moving her lips against his, and as a reward Erik took her to new heights.

He licked the seam of her lips, triggering a breathless moan from her. She felt his tongue again, and when she parted her lips he slipped his tongue inside her mouth, coaxing a hum of satisfaction from her.

He teased her relentlessly, licking inside her mouth only to pull back and repeat the action all over again, as if this was some game, a source of amusement for him when it only left her wanting more.

She could not touch him, could not drag him closer. Her hands were still clasped behind her, and her body still pressed between his and the wall. Mya could not even pull her head away from the grasp he had on her hair, and every tug when she tried both frustrated and exhilarated her.

Erik was in control of this entire experience, and while she loved that she could surrender to him, she also wanted to give him something, to show him and herself she could bring him the same pleasure he brought her. So, when he left her mouth, a strand of saliva being the only thing that connected the two of them, and then returned, she opened her mouth, caught his lower lip, and sucked.

Erik's body tensed, straining against hers, so Mya did it again. This time her canines caught the skin of his lip. They were still sharp, sharper than she was used to, and without meaning to she cut his lip open. Two droplets of blood entered her mouth, dripping onto her tongue.

A tremor passed through her entire body, and although she knew it might be wrong— that she had never asked Erik's permission to drink his blood—she could not stop herself from tasting him, from sucking his blood into her mouth.

The moan that left her was loud and sinful, and Erik's own groan of pleasure turned what was once something of shocking passion into a turbulent chasm of war. His hands left the grip he had on her hair to wrap themselves around her. She took him, took his weight, his taste, and she craved every ounce of it more than air itself.

Mya's hands wound themselves in the tresses of his golden hair, twisting and pulling, gripping like he had done to her, to show him what she needed, what she desperately desired: for him not to stop. All she could feel was Erik—the way he sucked her lips, how his tongue felt when he ran it across hers, how he tasted like mint and honied pears.

Mya loved it. She loved the shivers that coursed

through her body, the gooseflesh that puckered her skin, the way his lips seemed to transfer her whole body and soul to another dimension where only he resided.

Erik's hand slid up her back, and she moaned for him. He fisted her hair once more, bunching the strands and gripping them at her scalp as he kept her head tilted so he could kiss her deeper, more passionately, and she took every drop of what he gave.

Mya clung to him, her fingers digging into his shoulders and arms, feeling his muscles tense, tendons tighten and release, the way his chest shuddered each time she opened her mouth to his, each time he took another breath and breathed her in. She could feel how hard and fast his heart was beating, that it seemed to race just as quickly as hers. This was unforgiving, electrifying, and Mya could only succumb to the waves of pleasure that ignited her skin.

Her core grew wetter, her nipples so swollen and sensitive that every rub against her chemise was almost painful. Erik's erection pushed against her stomach, and the knowledge that he was so hard for her nearly made her weep. Mya knew he was large--she could tell that through his clothing--but the question of how he would fit inside her never crossed her mind. He would fit, and she would take him gladly. Mya expected the pain of having her virginity taken, but she would give it to him. She would take him with wild abandon, even if he split her in two, because this moment with him was worth everything.

Erik's teeth raked over her lip. There was a gentle sting, and then he tasted her, drank her blood like she had his. Euphoria filled her and she gasped at the heady feeling. Mya had drunk and exchanged blood plenty of times before, but this was different. It was as if her entire body was exploding cell by cell, molecule by molecule, shifting and changing, *accepting* Erik as a secret piece of her body that she had been missing all along. In her heart he had always been, and now her body demanded to be complete.

Erik heeded that call with a guttural groan. He lifted her, and she wrapped her arms tighter around him, grasping him. She refused to be separated from him even for a moment. With one hand he held her, bracing her against the wall, while the other slid down to her ankle, then up, taking her gown and chemise with it while the cold metal of his ring brushed her skin.

Mya shifted to help him raise her dress. When he tugged it to her waist, she wrapped her legs around him, crossing her ankles at his back. He groaned, guided her down just slightly and then pressed his clothed erection against her damp core.

She moaned so loudly into his mouth that someone was sure to have heard her, but it did not stop either of them. He did it again and again, guiding and pushing while he gripped and kneaded her behind. She circled her hips, brushing against him as he did her, and she delighted in the intensity of the shudders that racked his body. Erik's hand snaked up the back of her dress, and the cold air in contrast to the warmth of his large palm made her gasp.

He finally tore his mouth away from hers only to bring it lower. Erik kissed her jaw, then her neck, and Mya tilted her head back against the wall to give him access. She fisted his tunic, pulling at the material as she fought to feel his skin. She wanted to touch him, feel him bare against her, to leave her mark on him in the same way he was leaving his on her.

Erik kissed lower still, down to her breasts which heaved with every breath she took. He pulled at the material of her gown, but his finger slipped through a tear in the fabric.

The smell of blood that wafted from the shift of cloth hit them both, and they froze. That was where they had torn her gown that morning, a reminder of her assault. The memory hurt and angered her, but perhaps what was worse was the knowledge that she and Erik could not move past it, not like this, no matter how much she wanted to.

Mya reached to touch Erik's cheek, but he tilted his head away from her. The rejection stung, but she understood. Whatever the reason was this ... exchange had occurred, it was over and done with. Perhaps Erik had never meant for it to go this far in the first place.

Still, it crushed her heart when he said in a low voice, "Uncross your legs from me, Mya."

She blinked, embarrassed and disappointed that she clearly struggled to let him go, when he did not feel the same. Mya uncrossed her ankles from his back, but as she tried to lower her legs, he only pulled her closer, his grasp tight on her waist. Erik guided her to the ground, her descent a slow and blissful torture as Erik pressed into her. She brushed against his hips, thighs, calves, and ankles until her feet met the road. She was still so sensitive that she squeezed her eyes shut and bit her lip, trying to cover her moan.

"My apologies," Erik said, his voice gruff and hoarse. When Mya opened her eyes, he looked animalistic, feral. His cheekbones were sharper, the white of his skin now pink and flushed. His jaw was tight and his canines extended between his lips, but it was his eyes, the normal silver now red, that captivated her most of all.

Mya lifted her hand again to touch his face. This time he stilled so much that she could not even feel his chest move to breathe. She stopped, dropping her hand to his chest because the truth was right there in front of her. She may not know his feelings, but there was *something* there, and perhaps he struggled just as much as she did with letting go.

"No apology necessary," she whispered.

Erik released a harsh breath then braced his hand against the wooden wall. His fist tightened and extended several times and his entire body seemed to tremble before he said, "Who hurt you, *fagr skjaldmær min?* Tell me their names."

She tilted her head away from his, but he brought it back with a grasp of her chin.

"I do not want you to get involved," she said, her voice wavering under his intensity.

Erik's eyes narrowed, his face seeming to grow sharper as he bent down to her level. "I was bound to be involved the moment they came near you. They brought this fate upon themselves," he growled.

The deep predatory sound made her eyes widen, but it was the way Erik's hand stroked her chin, his fingers caressing her jaw gently as his eyes softened ever so slightly, that had her melting again.

"I will never hurt you, not you," he whispered as his eyes begged her to understand, to believe his words. "But I will kill whoever has done this to you."

"They are nobles," Mya hissed. "If they find out it was you—"

"I do not care."

"Erik!" she pleaded.

"I do not care!" he roared. "Nobles or not, they are a disgrace, a blight on this land. They do not deserve to breathe the same air as you. They should have never touched you. *No one* is allowed to touch you but me! You are *mine!*"

The words hung between them, suspended in the silence that was broken only by their rushed breathing.

Erik dropped his hand from her, and his face fell. "I—"

"I am yours, Erik"—Mya fiddled with the cloth of

his tunic, unable to meet his eyes—"in every sense of the word."

When she finally gathered her courage to look up, the look of shock on his face caused her to laugh even as a tear slid down her cheek. Erik caught the droplet with his thumb, wiping away the wetness from her cheek, and yet the heartbreak in his gaze caused another one to fall.

"You are a gift, *fagr skjaldmær min.* One that I do not deserve, and one that I cannot accept no matter how much I want to."

The arrow of heartbreak buried itself deeper in Mya's chest, but she nodded. Mya bit her lip, using the pain to keep the weight of her sadness from spilling over, and whispered, "If you cannot accept me or take me, I will never allow another the chance."

"Mya," he began, but she shook her head. Erik took a breath and rubbed her cheek again, his touch bringing a warmth that only hurt her more because of how much she craved it. "Let me do what I can for you. Let me protect you. Let me be your shield, your guard. Please," he begged when she did not answer.

In all the years she had known Erik, he had never once begged her. Convinced her? Yes. Toyed with her? Yes. But begged her? No. Resisting him was hard enough, but once the plea had passed his lips, she knew that there was nothing she would not give him.

Taking a deep breath, she said, "Gilbert and Randolph Bennet. Richard Browne. Walter Godfrey."

Simply saying their names brought her so much anxiety and disgust that bile rose up her throat. She swallowed it down and continued, knowing she had no other choice.

"I hurt Walter, and the other three saw me turn. Tubert and Albin tried to defend me, and that is when I ran away. I do not think they saw what I-I am." She shook her head as fresh tears came to her eyes. "I am sorry. I am so sor—"

"Shh," Erik whispered as he hugged her tightly, his warmth chasing at the coldness in her bones. "You have done well, *fagr skjaldmær min*. So, so well," he murmured into her hair.

"But the nobles, they saw me," she cried into his chest.

"That was unavoidable, *fagr skjaldmær min*. You did the best you could, far better than I would have." He pulled back just slightly, enough to wipe the tears from her eyes. "I never doubted you for a moment. Your bravery knows no bounds."

She shook her head. "I am not brave. I am not like you."

"No, *fagr skjaldmær min*, you are *better*. Now, I need to call on your bravery once more."

Erik grasped her arms, leading her away from the wall. He checked her cloak and tightened it around her, hiding the rips in her gown. "Can you make it home safely for me?"

"Yes, but they may have told someone by now. If they did, the church—"

Erik stroked her cheek with his palm. "Mya, do not worry about me. I can handle this. Even if they told the church, I would happily kill the members and send them to their new god if it means I can keep you safe for one more day. Now go," he ordered.

She knew there would be no more trying, reasoning, or attempts at convincing; Erik had made up his mind and was now on his mission, and there would be nothing she could do to stop it.

She took a few steps, then paused and turned back to him. "Come home to me," she said.

She did not hear his reply, but she swore she saw him mouth the words, "I could never stay away."

CHAPTER 4

Erik did not come home that night.

Mya waited for him in her room. When he did not come to her, she searched every room of the house. She even asked the staff if they had seen him, but everyone gave her the same story: Erik had left the grounds for an important meeting and would be back in due course.

That information should have made her feel more at ease, except Mya could not smell Erik's scent anywhere. His rooms were empty and his bed was made. There was not a single crinkle in the bed sheets or a curtain pulled back too far; nothing that would indicate someone had slept there. If he had not come home, who had given the household staff that message?

The only other people Erik trusted were Gregori and Lucas. But if he had spoken to them, how much had he told them? Mya did not believe Erik would have told them about yesterday's events, but it was possible they could have assumed what had happened. If they did not know and Mya went to ask them about Erik's whereabouts, they would pester her until she finally gave them the truth, and then both her brother and cousin would go on the same murderous rampage Erik was now on.

She did not want that. Mya wanted her family to live blissfully unaware of her troubles, and so she bit her tongue and held her curiosity. She would simply wait. While Erik often needed to go away for a week or two at a time, he always took staff with him and made ample preparations. This spontaneity was not like him, which meant it would only be a matter of time until the staff grew suspicious.

Another day came and went, and there was still no sign of Erik. Mya stayed awake the whole night awaiting his arrival, but he never entered their house. There was no creak of a floorboard, no whine of a door opening, no sudden breeze from a window. There was nothing.

The household staff gave Mya the same answer as the day before, and she was beginning to grow frustrated. She did not know where to turn. Not only was she worried about Erik, not sleeping had wreaked havoc on her metabolism. While a vampire did not need to eat or sleep, doing so allowed their body to enter a rested state where their metabolism would be better controlled. Without those, Mya needed to consume more blood, if she did not, it would be easier for her to lose control again.

That night she drank an extra cup of pig's blood and forced herself to settle down in bed, but her mind refused to calm, leaving her tossing and turning in a half-asleep state for hours. When she began to settle and finally drifted to sleep, she dreamed of warm arms wrapping around her.

"Shh, love," Erik said, his voice low and quiet. "Sleep now. I am with you."

A small smile graced her lips as he settled in behind her, the warmth of his chest seeping into her back and she further relaxed into his embrace.

The following morning, the sun shone brightly into her room, alerting her that she had slept well toward midday. She rolled over onto her back with a sigh. She knew the feeling of Erik sleeping beside her had simply been a dream, but it had felt so real, so deliciously perfect.

Tears rolled down her cheeks, the only release she could find for the weight of it all. Two days ago, her only concerns were unrequited love and a feeling of unbelonging. Now she was worried that the love of her life had fallen into chaos and possible ruin because of her, and beneath it all were the memories and emotions of that fateful day.

Rape was a common issue in England—and all over

the world, Mya assumed—but as far as she was aware, nobles were normally spared from experiencing such a thing. It was more usual among the commoners, simply because the rich could afford justice and the poor could not.

It sickened her that this was an accepted normality of their society, but after having gone through it she realized it was so much worse. Mya had been spared by her vampire nature. Yes, Tubert and Albin had attempted to help her, but what could a crippled man and his young son do against four nobles? They, much like Erik, were willing to risk their lives to help her, but what about all the women who did not have someone to do that for them?

Mya was not sure if stopping her rape before it happened was better or worse for her psyche. Did she really deserve to feel as though she was a victim of a crime that she was lucky to not fully experience, when there were those that had it so much worse? Was it any better when she now knew the outside world was not safe for her, that at any time she could be made to go through the same thing again?

She shook her head, harshly wiping away the tears at her eyes.

No, comparing her trauma and pain to someone else's would never get her anywhere, yet it still hurt. It still cut at something inside her to have to go through all of this in silence. If Erik had not been there, she would never have told him. She would never have told *anyone.* Her secret would have died with those men, and now, once again, she wished she had killed them.

Perhaps she should not be so villainous. Perhaps that was not what a young woman of her stature should think of as a resolution. Perhaps her morals were skewed because she was more monster than human, and yet, humans could be the most monstrous of all.

Mya sniffed and wiped the snot from her nose. Those men may have not raped her, but they had stolen something from her: the last remaining strands of her naivety. Any innocence she once had was now gone. Mya could only see this world for the darkness that lay inside of it, and she, just like every being on this planet, held some of that darkness.

When Erik returned, and he *would* return to her, even if she had to hunt him down and bring him back kicking and screaming, she would ask him to help her understand that darkness. She would tame it, use it, morph it for the future, because she would never be a victim again. Her life, regardless of how much it made her ache inside, was still her own, and she was done living by the laws of others that did not serve her. She had the power to save herself from any fate she chose, but she needed to learn that power, learn how to use it and harness it in a way that worked best for her. And once she did, she would use it for others as well, and to hell with anyone who stood in her way.

Mya sat up and squared her shoulders with determination. She took a deep inhale, intent on calming her inner thoughts, but instead she choked on the scent on her skin: pine, ash, smoke, and cinnamon. She froze, then in a flurry of movement, she twisted her nightgown and lifted it to her nose. On her next inhale, she sobbed in realization. She had not dreamed of Erik; he had been there. She held her pillow up to her nose and smelled him all over it. A shaky laugh escaped her as she hugged it close. He had come home to her! He was safe.

He was in my bed.

The thought made her cheeks warm, but then a chirp drew her attention to her window. Pale red curtains were dusted in swirls of beige and bronze and held open by beige tassels at the corners, revealing a matching sheer curtain which allowed the light to filter in. Mya never liked to close her curtains, preferring to fall asleep to the sight of the moon and wake to the sun. As she watched the light filter through the thin fabric, she noticed a small red ribbon trapped under her window, keeping it cracked open just enough to let the typical call of the birds sound than normal.

Mya knew with absolute certainty she had left her window closed last night.

So that is how he entered my room.

She padded over and lifted the window with a small smile, plucking at the piece of red ribbon. When it did not come away in her hand, she realized it was tied to an object. Tugging on it led her to a bundle full of herbs.

Mya breathed in the fragrances of lavender, sage, mint, lungwort, and rose, all the herbs she had bought from the apothecary on her last outing. She fell to her seat beneath the window and hugged the herbs to her chest, basking in the aroma and thoughtfulness behind the gift. The fact that Erik would go to such lengths when he realized how much this meant to her was overwhelming. She was in awe of his care and attention, and she had to force herself to breathe through the tender feelings it invoked.

She needed to see him, to thank him and talk to him about her thoughts and desires. But if Erik was nearby, why would he have used her window to come in and out of her room? Why would he have left the herbs for her to find, instead of bringing it to her directly? Something was amiss.

Mya pulled on her indoor clothes and ran out of her room to find him, but much like before he was nowhere to be found. No one knew of his exact whereabouts, nor were they concerned. Erik had left a letter before heading out once again, stating that he would be busy for several more days but would return as soon as he could.

The news crushed her. Not because she expected his attention or a personal letter but because she knew it was a lie. Erik had never left her alone for so long without speaking to her directly and explaining where he was going. This had to do with her, with her assault. She knew that like she knew her own name. The worry came rushing back, crashing into her, and fresh tears spilled down her face, because she knew the truth. Whatever had happened, whatever Erik had done, had now grown increasingly more complicated, and it was all her fault.

———

Three more days had passed, and with each one Mya feared she was losing her mind. More gifts had been left outside her window: a book she had been coveting regarding the study of physiology, more herbs—the kind that only doctors were allowed to purchase—and a letter.

She had read that letter more times than she could count, and yet she found herself sitting on the chair beside the window with it in her hand, reading his scrawled penmanship once again.

"*Mya,*

I hope these herbs will assist you in your experiments. I expect to hear about them when I return. Please do not worry. Make sure to eat and sleep regularly. I will be with you soon, fagr skjaldmær min.

With all my love,

Erik."

Mya rested her head against the window and sighed,

her breath fogging the glass as she tightened her grip on the letter.

Where are you? Are you hurt? Are you in danger? Why will you not let me see you, Erik? Why will you not tell me what has happened?

"Penny for your thoughts, little sister?"

Gregori's sudden presence made her jump in the chair. Mya clutched her racing heart, and while a smile appeared on her older brother's face, he did not laugh. That meant they were going to have a very serious and honest conversation, whether Mya wanted to or not. Still, she could at least try to speak half-truths.

"I am waiting for Erik to return home, that is all. Do you have any news on his arrival?"

"And who is to say he is not already here?" Gregori said with a smirk.

Mya's eyes grew wide. "He is? He has returned?"

Gregori stepped to the window, staring out into the distance. "How odd. Before Erik left, he gave me a series of instructions and messages to give the staff. But none were for you." He turned and his hazel eyes burned into her dark olive. "Why do you think that is?"

Mya's back straightened. Her eyes narrowed, but she continued to gaze out of the window. "I do not presume to know why Erik does or does not do something. Just as I do not know why he is not home. But you seem to, *brother*," she bit out.

Gregori took a chair and dragged it beside her, positioning the back toward her as he straddled the chair.

The action was so at odds with their noble personas that it calmed her, even if she knew his seemingly relaxed posture was nothing but a facade.

Gregori crossed his arms on the top of the chair and rested his chin on them as he studied her. Mya refused to back down from the challenge and stared right back into his eyes. It was futile, though, as it always had been and likely always would be.

"I think you know exactly why Erik left, and if you do not want to tell me then that means it has to do with you." Gregori straightened and grasped the chair hard in his fists, his posture reminding her of Erik. "What happened to you?"

Mya opened her mouth to speak, but her body betrayed her and she shuddered before the lie could slip between her teeth. It was only for a moment, but her brother saw it. His eyes grew just a tad in realization before narrowing. His nostrils flared as he asked again, "What happened, Mya?"

She shook her head. "Gregori, I love you even if you are a royal pain in my side, but this does not concern you."

He glared at her, so she hurried to continue. "The only reason Erik knows is because he was there. I am not willing to tell you anything further. Please let this go."

Gregori tapped on the chair, his movements growing stronger with each beat until she worried the wood was snap under his ministrations. Then he simply let go. His shoulders tensed and released multiple times until eventually he lifted his hand and ran it through his short brown hair.

For a moment he simply stared at her, eyes flashing between annoyance and disappointment, then he sighed.

"I do not like when you keep secrets from me. But you are old enough to know what is best for you. However, I need to know this. Was Erik the one who hurt you?"

Mya could not stop her brow from furrowing. "No, Erik would never hurt me," she said without a moment of hesitation.

Gregori nodded then tapped on the chair again, his gaze turning to the window as he stood. In the silence Mya wondered if he believed that if he gave her time, she might tell him everything, but she would not. She turned to stare out the window too, curious as to whether Gregori had seen something, hopeful that perhaps Erik was just beyond her view.

"I see everything that happens here," Gregori began. He glanced her way once more, then back to the window. "It is my job to see everything that happens here. It is my job to fill Erik's role in its entirety when he's gone."

Mya looked up at him. She knew her brother took on the responsibilities of the house when Erik was away, but for the first time she wondered what all that entailed. Mya was so busy hating and questioning her place in this world that she had never stopped to question her family's. Was Gregori happy? Were the responsibilities placed on him too much?

Again, she realized how much he looked like Erik. It was in his stance, his form. She knew Erik was a mentor and friend to her brother, but did Gregori feel like she did, obligated to play a role he did not want? What were his dreams, and when was the last time she had asked?

Gregori's voice drew her out of her thoughts. "When Erik left, he gave me messages and instructions for the staff. He then asked me to make sure that you were well."

His eyes roamed over her features before he crossed his arms and gripped them, fingers clenching a tad too tightly. "He would not tell me what happened to you, and you will not tell me what happened to you. I have to say, as your older brother I am quite hurt that neither of you trust me. But I understand that there are some things that even I cannot resolve."

Mya opened her mouth to reassure him, but he silenced her with his next words.

"Erik and I have a pact when it comes to you."

Mya tilted her head to the side, frowning. "A pact? What do you mean?"

"The day after we arrived here, Erik asked me for my permission to watch over you, to take care of you."

Mya's breath caught in her throat and her eyes widened.

Gregori chuckled. "I would have responded the

same way as you just did, except I saw how he looked at you. It is the same way that he has looked at you for years, and the same way that you have looked at him. I see the two of you, the way you are together. You are constantly drawn together like a moth to a flame, back and forth, to and from." He motioned with his fingers and sighed. "Although you never seem to act on that very apparent attraction, which saddens me. While I am incredibly protective of you, and perhaps slightly overbearing, I want you to be happy. It is for that reason that I gave Erik my approval, and it is the very same reason why I will give you the information I know you seek the most right now."

He turned to her, and she swallowed, hoping to wet her dry throat as her heart threatened to beat out of its cage.

"I hope that one day you will be able to trust me and tell me what happened to you."

Mya shook her head and grabbed her brother's arm. "It is not that I do not trust you. I just do not want—"

"I understand," he said, but Mya saw the hurt in his eyes, as if he had failed her in some way.

"Gregori, I trust you. I swear I do!"

"Perhaps you do in some things, but you do not trust me to take the correct actions. Maybe it is because you know me, and maybe you are correct. Maybe you are trying to protect me the same way I have tried to protect you. Still, without the knowledge of what you have suffered, I cannot attempt to assist you with your pain. I have created a space between us in which you do not feel that you can come to me."

He leveled her with his gaze. "I know that is why you did not ask me of Erik's whereabouts when you knew I would know the answer."

If it was possible Mya would have made herself as small as a mouse and scurried away from that gaze, because her brother was correct. She did not trust him, but it was not because he had done anything to her. She realized now that it was because she did not trust herself, and as such could not trust others completely.

"I hope that one day that will change," Gregori said. He squeezed her hand and patted it gently before lowering it to her lap. Then his voice grew firmer, although tinged with a sliver of sadness. "At the southeast edge of the property lies a large oak tree wrapped in ivy. It is near a large field of clover. Do you know it?"

Mya knew by his voice that their conversation was coming to a close, so she nodded.

"Good. Cross the clover field into the woods. Continue through the woods until you hear a river. Make sure to keep it on your right. From there you will see a cabin. That is where Erik is staying."

Gregori watched her, waiting, and she gave a single nod of understanding.

"Settle whatever this is between the two of you. Once you have," he said, his voice softening, "come and talk to me. Can you do that for me, little sister?"

"Of course," she murmured.

Gregori dropped a kiss on her forehead and tucked a wiry strand of hair behind her ear. "Go at night. If I do not see that you have returned by the morning, I will go and find you. Please, whatever you do, return. I do not want to have to chase after you and find you both ... indecent."

"Gregori!" she objected, but he was already walking away, his laugh echoing down the hall at her blush.

CHAPTER 5

The cabin was well hidden in the forest, under a deep canopy of trees and surrounded by brush. Ivy and vines grew along its sides, as if the forest was trying to reclaim it. If it were not for her enhanced senses and her brother's instructions, Mya would have missed it entirely.

When she had first set out for the cabin, Mya wondered what she might find, debating whether the cabin might be decrepit and cold. As soon as she saw it, she felt a rush of admiration for Erik's skill. The cabin might appear abandoned to others, but Mya knew better. It was lush and wild. It was *alive*. It was clear that Erik loved this place and took great care of it, and Mya felt a sense of honor in knowing its location.

She walked up the steps and paused at the door. Mya could not smell Erik in the cabin or the surrounding area, which meant there was a possibility he had laid a trap at the door to ensure no one entered while he was away. Still, she had to try. She was a vampire and could heal quickly should anything happen, and she was certain that he would come to her aid immediately if she triggered anything that could hurt her.

She tried the door and found it unlocked, so she opened it slowly. Relief washed over her when nothing exploded or hurled itself at her face. Surveying the room, Mya found a hearth, bed, basin, wooden storage chest, a small table, lantern, and a chair. Several of the furnishings appeared handmade. Had he built and furnished this place himself? How often did he use it as a quiet retreat? Was this why he always smelled of the forest?

Mya mulled over those questions, realizing she had far too many now, and decided to light the lantern while she sat and waited for Erik to return.

As time went by, her emotions grew, but none more so than the nervousness at Erik's reaction to seeing her. She was concerned that perhaps he had not only stayed away due to complications with protecting her, but that he may have been avoiding her as well. Yes, they had crossed a line neither of them could return from, but Erik had always sought her out in the past. Still, what if he regretted everything and that was why he had stayed away, because he did not know how to communicate that to her?

She shook her head. Something in her screamed that was not the reason. But then what else could be the cause? Mya was so inexperienced and unprepared for this situation, and it frustrated her. She gripped her gown, nails biting into the material, and decided it did not matter what the reason was. She would wait here for as long as it took to get the answers to her questions, and she would not give up until she did.

She had spent the past five days rationalizing Erik's actions and trying to understand everything that had happened, but it was all too much too soon. As she sat in the light of the lantern, Mya thought of her life and her choices. She analyzed what she was proud of and pictured what she hoped to achieve. She thought of her brother, of how much she loved and adored him and of the weight on his shoulders. She wondered if her cousin had the same weight or if he had been spared some of the responsibility by being the youngest between the three of them.

Then her thoughts turned to Erik, of how much he must have gone through to create the life he had. There was much she did not know about him, but that thought did not diminish her feelings toward him. In fact, it strengthened them. But just as she felt wonderment toward Erik, she felt guilty for not already having the answers to the secrets he kept.

She wanted to know those secrets, but had she ever truly asked? Mya reasoned that she could not ask what she did not know, but that was not entirely true. The truth was, as foolish as it may be, she was jealous of the years she had not known Erik. Those years had helped to make him into the man he was today, the man she loved completely, and yet she was jealous of the influences that had created that man, of the time other beings—both immortal and human—had spent with him, of those he may have cared for or even loved before her.

It was selfish and stupid, but it was how she felt nonetheless. She had to acknowledge those feelings honestly. She *wanted* to know Erik's secrets, his thoughts, his past, because she wanted to understand him and to know him in all ways.

As she looked around the cabin, taking in its simplicity, she wondered if Erik felt the same lack of balance she did. They lived in something akin to a castle, and yet he had a cabin hidden away from prying eyes. Did he crave the separation from the lies that embroidered their lives in the same way she did?

A soft click brought her focus back to the room. It was a sound no animal or insect could make, and her breath stalled in her chest. A moment later the door opened, and there Erik stood like a shadow, a creature of the night.

He did not move when he saw her, but she could feel his eyes on her even as he refused to meet her own. Then he entered the cabin, closed the door behind him and walked past her as if she did not exist.

"You should not be here, Mya."

It hurt that those were his first words to her. Her temper peaked but she swallowed it back, her need for answers more important than anything else. Instead,

Mya observed and waited. She studied his back, took in his blond hair, now stained with flecks of red. She could smell the scent of blood rolling off him as he moved toward the basin, and when he turned, she saw that his tunic was covered in it. Seeing her staring, Erik ripped off the material as if it had offended him in some way and it on the floor.

His anger did not scare her. This was Erik, *her* Erik. He had the same wide shoulders and muscled back, the same nipped waist and long legs, thick and sturdy like tree trunks. Underneath the smell of blood and dirt was his same unique scent, and in that she found comfort and courage.

She stood. Erik tensed and she came near, but she paid him no mind. Standing beside him at the basin, she inspected the front of his body, finding more blood there than anywhere else. It was undeniably human and came from someone who she was certain was no longer with this world.

She ripped a piece of her gown. Erik's eyes fixed on her, but Mya did not meet them. Instead, she wet the piece of cloth and held it to the back of his hand, wanting to help clean him. She needed to touch him, to connect with him and bridge the distance between them somehow.

"Do not," he warned, his voice exasperated, tired and longing, almost as if he felt the same way she did.

"Let me," she replied. Without waiting for his response, Mya placed her hand on his chest, and he allowed her to guide him to the side so that she could begin her task. She cleaned his fingers, then around his ring, his palm, his wrist, and the back of his hand. When all that was left was white skin, she asked, "Whose blood was this?"

"That is not of your concern."

While his words were curt, his tone lacked any force behind it.

"I did not wait five days and four nights for you, tossing and turning and wondering when you would come back home to me, and then walk all the way here for you to keep more secrets from me," she huffed.

Erik swallowed hard. Mya forced herself to take a shaky breath before she spoke again, trying once more to temper her anger. "In our ... companionship—"

"We are companions now?" Erik growled, the muscles in his arms clenching under her touch.

Mya's hackles rose. His stubbornness got under her skin and irritated her until she both wanted to kiss him and hit him. She forced herself to grip his wrist to stop from doing either.

"What else would you like me to call us? Do we have a relationship or are you going to continue to run away from me, to hide from me like a coward? I appreciate your gifts and your attempts at protecting me, but you were supposed to come home to me!"

He glowered at her. "Do not *ever* call me a coward again. I did come home to you! I simply—"

"Made sure to leave before I would see you."

He was quiet then, his arm limp in her grasp.

"Are you avoiding me?" she asked, her voice as soft as a whisper.

"I was..." he began, and then he grew silent.

She nodded, moving her attention to his other arm. "I have had a lot of time to think while you were away," she said, laughing coldly. "All I have been doing is thinking."

"Mya," he croaked. She knew he was pleading with her to understand something he refused to share, but it only angered her more.

"I have thought about what happened, about what it means. I have thought about how I feel about everything. I have thought about us and the times and history we share."

Erik was brimming, vibrating, and the tremors made her meet his silver eyes once more. They were shining so brightly, a startling, glowing silver that meant he was on the verge of falling into his vampire nature. Mya found it odd to think that it may be because of her, that she had that much power over him, that she could make him lose control simply with words, with breath, with her touch on his skin. It lit something in her, knowing his emotions may be so tied into her body that the connection they shared would start a war in his.

Then he asked, "Will you tell me what you have thought of?"

She nodded and lowered the cloth. Swallowing the thick ball of emotion in her throat, she gently placed her hands on his chest. Mya stared at the spot, relishing the warmth of his skin beneath her palms where his heartbeat strongly.

"Erik, I have been unhappy for a long time."

"I know," he whispered. His arms lifted as if to encircle her before falling to his sides again. She glanced at him and saw the look of defeat in his eyes. "I have tried to make you happy, but—"

"It was not for you to try. It was for me to try to understand everything in this world, to find my place in it. I have felt ... jilted by life. I have lost my home, my family. I do not understand this society, and I am treated horribly for the crime of being a woman. I have no power. I cannot study or learn the things I wish to in order to create a career or name for myself."

Mya shook her head. "Everything we are is a lie, even down to your last name. Do you know how long I have wished I could call you Erik Haraldsen?"

Erik lifted his hand to her cheek and lightly caressed her. Then he tucked her hair behind her ear and followed the wild curled strands down her back, drawing her closer and whispering into her ear, "And do you know how often I wish I could call you so many things?"

His simple touch whisked her tension away so quickly, she had to bite her lip to keep it from quivering. Taking a shaky breath, she said, "I understand it is not only for human protection but for our own. I understand that myself, Gregori, and Lucas are not strong enough to defeat hordes of humans. We are too young as vampires, and while we could win against perhaps five or ten or fifteen humans together, we could not defend ourselves against the entire town. I understand, truly I do, but I wish at the very least that we could have been honest with one another."

Another tremor swept through him. Erik pulled her closer, as if he hoped to use his body to stave off her concerns. "I have seen you sad and angry. I have seen your hate, yet I have never known how to fix it. Tell me how I can fix it. Whatever it is, I swear I will do it."

Mya looked up at him, eyes blurry by tears she refused to let slip. "Be honest with me, for once. Let me see you, learn about you, understand you in all the ways I have yet to. I, in return, will be honest with you. Starting right now."

She took a deep breath and let it out, squared her shoulders, and fought to keep her voice steady. "When those four men attacked me, my hatred overtook me. That was why it was so easy for me to succumb to my vampire nature. I *wanted* to hurt them. Not only because I was a vampire, but because I hated them just as I hated this world. That startled me. It *scared* me. I have never felt that way before, or perhaps I have always felt that way and I simply stowed the feeling away."

Mya took another deep breath, and her hands grasped Erik's broad shoulders. "But I cannot live my life that way. If I do, something will eventually happen again."

Erik's eyes burned into hers. "That will never happen. I will *never* let that happen to you again."

"You do not know what the future holds. Rape occurs all the time, all across these countries. Women are raised to endure it, sold to their kings, to their emperors and their lords to pleasure them in whatever way they require *whenever* they require it. The only thing that has protected me from that fate has been your status. But after that happened..."

She trailed off and shook her head to clear her thoughts. "I understand that I can protect myself, but only if I know myself. I do not want to lose myself to hatred again. I have lost time, Erik. I have lost time with my family, time enjoying my life, time with ... you. I wanted to kill those boys, Erik. I should be upset or disgusted at myself for that, and yet I feel nothing but pride. In that moment I was finally able to have the power to complete an action that was entirely my own."

Erik pulled her head to his, bending to meet her midway and level his gaze with her own. His next words were said gently, carefully. "Those boys, their deaths were warranted. But it should have never been on you. It should have never gotten to this. You know that. Tell me you do."

Mya nodded. "I do, but I still want to learn what you did. I want to learn how to defend myself. I wanted to kill them, and I hate that you were able to take their lives when I could not. That truth, that knowledge, has left a stain on my soul. Erik, how many women hurt this way? How many children are stolen from their homes? How entitled are the rich of this world allowed to be?" She squeezed his shoulders tightly, begging him to see her, to understand. "My soul craves vengeance, Erik. I need this taste of independence. Please, teach me how to fight."

He shook his head, his voice tight as if pained. "Mya—"

She refused to hear him decline, instead deciding to push him harder. "I need you to teach me how to fight and how to work through this, because I will put all of us at risk if it ever happens again. I will lose control, Erik, we both know that. You have kept our vampire abilities and power a secret from me. I know you have done that for a good reason. I know I am not responsible. I know I am not reliable like my brother or a jovial entertainer like my cousin. I have far too much darkness in me for that. It is easy for me to be angry—"

"Because you have a reason to, *fagr skjaldmær min!* Do not belittle yourself." Erik squeezed her, clutching at her back. "Your life is not as fair as ours. The life of a woman in these times is not easy. The troubles you face are terrible. You are allowed to feel the way you do, and I would be surprised if you did not. I wish you could see that. I wish you were not so hard on yourself."

Mya's arms flew through the air, then slapped down at her sides as her anger burst out of her. "I am hard on myself because I do not understand where I belong! I do not understand my strengths or my weaknesses. I do not understand any of it. You have given me preferential treatment for … whatever reason you have, but that is no longer enough, Erik. Show me how to fight as you showed my brother and cousin, or I will learn how to do it myself, but I guarantee I will make a mistake without you."

A tic started in his jaw, and he averted his eyes from hers.

Mya lowered her voice, begging, pleading, all anger gone. "I want to be better than this. I am so tired of feeling weak and not good enough. I believe that if I can at least find a way to gather strength, to explore my anger in a healthy environment with someone that I trust"—she cupped his chin and his gaze met hers—"I will feel comfortable enough to be vulnerable, to be better, more alive, more appreciative. I do not just want to be angry like this world is angry, Erik."

He sighed and hugged her to him once more. "Mya, I will always do anything that you ask me, whether I should or not."

"Thank you," she murmured into his chest.

For a while they stayed that way, holding and swaying against one another until Erik whispered, "Tell me what else you thought of."

Mya felt Erik's body tighten against her own as if he was preparing himself for some sort of battle. She bit her lip. "Am I right to assume that you only kissed me as a distraction against my vampire nature?" she asked quietly.

Erik remained silent, and that silence ate away at Mya's heart. She could feel it pounding against her body, blood roaring and pumping furiously through her veins.

"Tell me, *please,*" she begged. "I cannot continue to just stand here wondering—"

"It is not the only reason."

His confession was quiet, and yet it seemed to echo in her ears.

"Then why did you kiss me?"

"Do not make me have this conversation with you, Mya."

"We have to!"

"Mya."

His tone made her stop, the absolute dread and fear within it making her abandon everything, even breathing. In all the years she had known Erik, she had never once heard him sound afraid. He took a worried breath, one that she mimicked.

"I worry that if I tell you why, you will never look at me the same way again," he said finally.

A memory surfaced in Mya's mind, like the missing piece of a puzzle. "Is that why you told me you do not deserve me, even though I am yours?"

Erik nodded. When he met her eyes, she saw they were glazed over. In them was nothing more than a heartbroken man.

CHAPTER 6

It was as if the words were torn from him so breathlessly, so regrettably.

"I kissed you because I want to, constantly. I want you, always. I want you in a way that is uncontrollable, irreversible, infinite. But I cannot have you, Mya."

Mya shook her head and placed her hands on his chest, hoping she could somehow grasp onto him and shake him from his reasoning. "Tell me why. I may be blind to many things, but I am not blind to the way you are with me. I think you feel the same way about me as I do about you, so—"

"I do," he admitted.

"Then why—"

"Because you do not know my past, Mya!" Erik roared, ripping himself away from her to pace the wooden floor. "I protected you from it, from me! You do not know." He shook his head and changed direction, pacing faster, his boots sounding like a stampede against the floorboards even as his voice grew softer. "You do not know."

His outburst did not shock her, because she felt his pain. "Erik," she said carefully, "the last person I need protection from is you."

He froze and turned to her. "That is where you are wrong."

Mya took a step toward him, but he turned away from her once more. Eyes fixed on the door, he said deeply, "Sit down. Sit down and I will tell you about my horrid past. Maybe then you will finally understand why I do not deserve your love or your heart, nor a single shred of your mind." Erik held his shaking hand to his face, then shoved it roughly through his hair. "Possibly not even your trust, no matter how much I long to be deserving of it."

Mya reached out for him, her hand wavering in the air, then stopped herself. She had fought so hard to get him to speak about this. He looked so broken and she knew this would be the only time he would ever give her these answers. She needed them, *they* needed them.

Mya ignored the voice within her that begged her to reach out for him, touch him, soothe him with her skin, and instead turned and sat on the edge of the bed. She positioned herself where she could track his movements if he continued to pace. Then she did her best to brace herself for whatever pain weighed so heavily on Erik's heart, because no matter what he thought, she would help heal that pain. She would always be there for him, and she was certain nothing could change her mind.

Erik was a desperate, frantic mass of energy that could not be released. Many times he stopped, looked at Mya, and opened his mouth, only to shake his head and resume battering the floorboard of the cabin. Just as Mya was about to break the electric silence, Erik grabbed the wooden chair and bowed his head. He closed his eyes and took several deep breaths. When he finally spoke, he did not raise his head.

"There are two things that are needed to turn someone: a want for survival or desire for vampirism, and the blood of a vampire."

He gripped the chair harder. "I was accidentally turned in the middle of a war that I had been honor-bound to fight in but knew I would not survive. Myself, my father and many of the males in our village set out for this battle, fully aware we may not return home. In the end, I had to watch them die."

Mya bit her lip hard to keep herself from interrupting, even as Erik's misery coated the cabin and the distance between them in an unwavering sea of darkness.

"No one was alive when I came back as ... this." He gestured to himself before returning his hands to the back of the chair. "No one taught me how to be a vampire. I ... made horrible, *unforgivable* mistakes."

Erik shuddered. "I did not know how to control my

blood lust. I did not know how to feed properly. I did not know about animal blood. I was turned into a vampire in the middle of a raging war where blood *soaked* the ground, so I gorged myself on it. Then that battle ended, while my blood lust remained. After a while, I lost consciousness. I was closer to a village than I should have been for the inhabitants' safety."

He licked his lips nervously and his hands tightened on the chair, the wood creaking in his grip. "I hid out in the forest, terrified of what I was. I tried to kill myself, but nothing worked. Then I became hungry again. I did my best to keep away from people, I swear I did." His eyes met hers, filled with sorrow and damnation, before sliding away. "But the armies of our enemies, those that killed me, killed my people, were pillaging the villages, spilling more blood. The scent of it drove me mad, and I gorged myself on it again. Then I discovered desire."

Mya whispered his name, terrified of where this story would lead, but he was lost to the call of his horrible memories.

"There were women in the village that had escaped into the woods, and I-I..."

Mya pushed herself from the bed. In two strides she was beside Erik, her fingers catching the tears that fell from his eyes just as he said, in barely more than a whisper, "I hunted them. I raped them, Mya."

Erik pulled away from her. "You know now what it is to lose yourself to your blood lust. How you are there in your mind but not in control of your body." His Adam's apple bobbled in the lantern light as he swallowed. "I remember their faces. I remember their cries. I remember how many people I killed while lost to my blood lust."

Mya covered her mouth to keep her own cries at bay, as tears—tears for him, for them—streamed down her face.

"This went on for fifty years, Mya. I could not find another vampire or immortal. No one helped me. I tried to talk to the medicine men, the physicians of those times, but they could not help me. I tried to lock myself away, but my chains were never strong enough. I employed pirates, mercenaries, the strongest people I could find in the hopes that they may be able to subdue me. It never worked, and when I freed myself, I killed every one of them. For fifty years I tried to control my blood lust, and failed."

She cupped his cheeks. "What made you stop?"

He looked at her, his eyes drowning in despair. "A little boy who screamed and threw stones at the monster who was raping and butchering his mother. That face—"

Erik shook his head as if he were trying to clear the memory, then pushed away from the table and sat down on the bed, hands clasped between his knees. "That face will haunt me for the rest of my days. When I needed to feed, I used the abhorrence in his expression to make me regain control. I continued to use it until I was able to grasp my limits."

Erik gulped, breathed, and looked down at his hands, as if questioning if they were capable of nothing but destruction. "I have kept track of that boy, the man he became, and the subsequent generations of his family all this time. I have donated whatever they have needed, and I will continue to do so until I am no longer on this planet, but that will still never be enough. I ripped that little boy's life apart in front of him because I could not control myself."

A bitter smile flashed on his face as he looked at her, and it broke her heart. "I am not someone you should trust, Mya. I am not worthy of your love. I am a despicable and horrible person. The things I have done are atrocious. I am no different than the monsters that tried to rape you only a few short days ago."

Mya moved toward him, intent to hold him, to stop his words, but Erik ignored her. "And if you could so foolishly believe in me even after all of this"—his voice broke as more tears streamed from his eyes—"it still would not matter, because I must do the best I can to ensure that you and your brother and your cousin will not go through the same pain that I have. You must understand our metabolisms, our powers, our weaknesses, how we must fight to remain calm, how we must have an outlet for our rage. You must understand everything so that you will never face what I have or do what I have done, so you will never be the monster inside a little boy's story."

Mya braced the chair as she felt her world shift, leaving her spinning and choking under Erik's sea of turmoil.

"Do you understand that if I slack in my duties, if I have a distraction, if anything in our world ever goes wrong, I have failed you all?" Erik pressed at his eyes with his palms, then raked his fingers through his hair. Then he whispered, "And do you understand that even though I know all of this, that I feel all of this, I still want you? That no matter how impossible it should be, you are still there? You are underneath my skin, pumping through my very veins, Mya! I am supposed to be impartial to the three of you, and yet if you, your brother, and your cousin were in peril, I would always come to your aid first, whether I should or not. You are my distraction, my weakness, and I cannot stop it. I cannot control this. I cannot resist *you*. I cannot think or be any other way."

Erik stood in one fluid motion, his eyes flashing. Mya reached for him, but the distance seemed impenetrable.

"I cannot become distracted, Mya. If I do, not only will people die but I could lose all of you. I could lose *you*. And even if you do not die, you may fall into the same peril that rots away at my soul."

He took a deep breath, his eyes telling her of his conclusion before the words could leave his mouth.

"I take care of the people here because I have the power to. I protect them because I should, but I know that nothing I do will ever make amends for the lives I have taken. So, you see, Mya, I am not a good man. I am not right for you."

Mya heard his words. She heard his story, his pain, his terrible nightmare, and she saw him differently. It was just as Erik said it would be, except instead of a monster she saw him as someone who needed her just as much as she needed him. He needed her heart, her love. He needed her to accept his past, to love him in his present, and to grow with him through his future.

Perhaps she was foolish, or perhaps it was because she remembered how it felt to lose control of herself to her vampire nature, to want to kill, to unleash her rage upon the land. The man Erik had become when he lost himself all those years ago was not the man he was today. But that man, that sad, unfortunate soul, had been forced to carry his sins on his own. She did not want that for him any longer.

Mya approached him. He tried to back away, to create space between them, but she would not let him. When he could go no further, Mya stood on the tips of her toes and wrapped her arms around his shoulders, the position difficult and awkward as Erik stood straight and stiff, a marble statue in her embrace. Then he gripped her arms and tried to remove them, but she refused and tightened her grip. Erik moved his hands down, gripping her sides, pushing her back, but again she refused to move.

"Mya," he croaked, "leave me, please."

"I will not. I will never leave you."

"Mya—"

"Let me love you, Erik. You have spent so long hating your life. Open yourself up to me. Let me comfort you."

"I do not deserve your comfort," he whispered.

"I decide the pieces of me that someone receives, Erik, and I want you to have them all. Just as I hope to one day hold all of yours." She squeezed her arms tighter around his neck, grasping her forearms to keep him close to her. "No one helped you during that dark time, so let me help you now. You told me you could not deny me, so do not try to do so now. Let me share the weight of your burdens and worries. Let me bring you the same peace you have brought me all these years. I am right here with you. I am not going anywhere. I will always be right here by your side. You will never be alone again," she whispered.

A breath left him, and with it he succumbed to her, his final barrier broken. Erik crumbled, his shoulders sagging against her, then his knees. Suddenly they were both on the ground, she within his lap with his arms circling her as they clung to one another. As his head leaned against her shoulder, she thought about her life, and the lives of her brother and her cousin. What would they have endured if Erik had not been with them?

What would have happened if they had been turned accidentally too? At least they would have had one another, but Erik had no one.

Mya understood that he had done terrible, despicable things, but she also understood that he would have never committed those atrocities in his right mind. To her, he was not the problem nor the solution; he was as much a victim as the people who had lost their lives to him.

Mya wished that she could wipe away Erik's every fear, every dreadful misdeed, but she could not. Still, from now on she would try as hard as she could to remind him of exactly how she saw him.

She took a deep breath as her hands moved to his back, kneading his muscles. "I know how negatively you think of yourself now, but I need you to know that I do not see you that way."

He tensed, but she continued. "You saved my life. You saved my family's lives. You were walking through the Black Death searching for people you could save. You were willing to take on the responsibility of another person's life, their choices and mistakes. You were willing to teach them, fend for them, and protect them. You have protected an entire town from hardship and worry."

"But that will never make up for what I have done," he whispered.

Mya nodded. "It does not need to make up for what you have done. The past is the past."

Erik shook his head in her neck. "It is not that simple."

She held him a little closer, a little tighter. "Maybe it can be if you believe you deserve forgiveness. You were a victim too, Erik."

He did not speak again, but his hold on her tightened as he buried his face deeper in her neck. When Erik's breathing had regulated and his muscles had relaxed, Mya kissed his hair and ran her fingers through the strands, working to untangle the ones matted with blood. When she had finished, she kissed his head, his temple, the corner of his eye. She breathed in his scent, basked in his warmth, and even though so much had transpired in such a few short hours, her heart glowed with the knowledge that he here, in her arms.

Erik was her home, and she wanted nothing more than to be the same for him, but she knew she could not give him what he needed most: forgiveness. Her words could never replace those of the people he killed, but perhaps her touch could help soothe his pain, even for a moment.

Mya kissed his head, his temple, the corner of his eye once more, and then followed the contours of his face. She kissed his regal cheek, his straight nose, and slid her lips back and down to his jaw. There she trailed her lips even as the hairs of his beard tickled her mouth.

Erik let out a long breath against her neck, raising goosebumps along her skin. They sat in each other's embrace for minutes, perhaps hours, until the comfort gave way to something darker, hungrier. And even though it was wrong, the feeling was undeniable.

Mya lifted her head, as did Erik. She met his eyes, taking in their depth, their intensity, and then she stared at his lips. She needed to feel them again, *desperately*. She cupped his face, her eyes flickering back to his just once, as if asking for permission. When she realized he would not pull away from her, she kissed him.

His lips were warm, soft and smooth against her own. She meant the kiss to be gentle, something just to taste, to stave off the hunger that had built between them, but then Erik pushed into her, claimed her lips for himself, and she was lost. Her fingers wound in his hair, gripping the strands, keeping him close just as his fingers gripped and pressed into her back.

He kissed her firmly, deeply, as if she were the water that quenched his thirst. This was not like the kiss in the alley. It was too passionate, too thorough, too intimate. It was as if there was nothing separating them— no time, no space, no air. Their bodies moved together, clinging to one another. She scratched his back and pressed her nails there, needing more of him as he moved her closer, pressing her hips against his as he squeezed her waist, her shoulders, then tangled his hand in her hair at her scalp.

Erik angled her head to deepen the kiss, and she moaned into his mouth. The sweep of his tongue lit her aflame, and her hips jerked involuntarily against his own, seeking him, pushing for them to be so close that nothing could separate them, nothing could break them.

Erik pulled at her gown, bunched the material around her waist and gripped her upper thigh. She panted against his mouth as his tongue played with hers. He devoured her, then he spread his legs, forcing her to sink more into his lap. When he gripped her hips once more, she rubbed herself against his erection. Lightning flashed through her body, causing her to moan his name.

Her voice woke them from the spell.

Erik pulled back to look at her, his eyes raking over her face and body like a caress. "We should stop," he croaked.

She nodded, unable to speak, but then he drew her to him and whispered, "One more," before crushing his lips to hers again.

This kiss was forceful, brutish, rough, a mass of lips and teeth and tongues, and she loved it. His fingers played at the laces of her gown as he began to undo them, then his hand slid up her back, skin to skin, while she guided her core against his erection, once, twice, earning a tortured moan.

"No more," he said, his voice hoarse. "No more."

Mya searched his eyes, scanned his face, and then she lifted her hands to his cheeks and caressed them, trying to convey everything she felt but did not know how to say. He grabbed hold of her wrists and brought her hands to his mouth, kissing the insides of her palms. Then he lifted her and carried her to his bed, where he sat her down carefully and looked her over once more. His fingers traced several spots of blood on her gown, and he sighed.

"I apologize for ruining your gown. Let me get you one of my tunics."

Before he could move, Mya grabbed his hand and kissed his palm. "Thank you."

The look he gave her was incredulous, as if she had just procured the known stars in the sky and delivered them to him. Then Erik moved to the wooden chest. Picking out a light-colored tunic, he offered it to her and she stood, accepting the cloth.

He swallowed hard. "Do you require any assistance getting changed?"

She did not—he had already undone the laces, and the five buttons on her gown were ones she had fastened herself that morning—but she would not miss a chance to have Erik's hands on her again. "Yes, please."

Mya turned, and Erik swept her hair over her shoulder. His hands paused on her back for a moment before sliding down slowly. He followed the curve of her spine with a brush of his knuckles, and the cold metal of his ring made her shiver.

He neared the bottom of her laces, undid the first button, and then chuckled. "You could have done this yourself."

She smiled. "I could have, but you so graciously offered."

He undid the last button, and his hands found themselves on her hips. He squeezed her and whispered in her ear, "Do not test me, Mya. You do not know what it will make me do to you."

She tilted her head back to his. "But I have enjoyed everything you have done to me thus far," she said. She caught his gaze and his blazing eyes reignited the fire in her core.

"Get dressed," he commanded before striding outside the cabin, leaving her to grin to herself.

Mya removed her gown and chemise, then changed into Erik's tunic which fell to her knees. For a single moment she stood in the cabin alone, her arms wrapped around her torso as she basked in his scent that was so embedded in the cloth that she was sure it would never completely come out. Then she moved to the hearth and threw her clothes into it.

Her body shook with a mixture of misery and anger when she thought of the night's events. So much life had been lost, so much death had occurred, so much injustice. Although the day had tested her more than she could ever have imagined, Mya felt that she understood Erik on a new level. She felt closer to him, more deeply rooted and connected in an indescribable way.

But she also felt the weight of his history, of his dark past. She shook her head again, took a shaky breath, and rolled her shoulders. It would never happen again.

She would not let it. Erik deserved better, and she would do everything she could to make him believe he was worthy of it. He needed to move forward, to let go of the past, and she would show him the way.

Mya moved to the door and opened it, the creak causing Erik to turn around. When he saw her, she watched his eyes begin to light, turning from their normal silver to something unnatural, predatory. It made her blush, and she could feel the tension between them like heat in the air.

"W-Would you like to get changed?"

Erik blinked, clearing away the spell. He looked down at his shirtless body and then nodded sharply. Mya moved onto the porch, but Erik urged her back inside.

"I will change outside."

"But—"

He shook his head. "I will wash the rest of the blood off in the river then change," he said, before gathering a fresh set of clothes for himself.

"Will you toss your bloodied clothes in the hearth? I have already put my gown there, and I would like to set a fire and burn them to remove any trace of evidence."

Erik's fingers stilled for a moment, then he gave her a smile so dazzling she felt weak at her knees. He stepped before her and dropped a kiss on her head. "That is an excellent plan, *fagr skjaldmær min.* I will be back to you shortly, and we can set a fire then."

When Erik returned, his clothes joined hers in the

hearth. They stood together, her arm wrapped around his waist, and his around her shoulder. Erik took a deep breath, filling his lungs with air. Mya watched his eyes flash orange, and when he exhaled, flames shot from his mouth. They filled the hearth, quickly eating away at their bloodied clothing. Mya hoped that one day, much like the clothes which curled and burned to ash under the intensity of the heat, so would the remnants of their negative pasts, never to be seen or experienced again.

CHAPTER 7

They watched in silence as the fire continued to dance before them, then Mya looked up at Erik, her dark olive eyes meeting his silver.

"Tell me what you did to the men that attacked me. Tell me how much of their blood you spilled."

One breath passed, then another and another as Mya waited for Erik's next words. She watched him, the twinge in his brow, the tightening and relaxing in his jaw, as if he was trying to plan his thoughts in an order that would be respectful to her.

She did not want respect. That form of politeness and modesty did not match her. She wanted brutal honesty, the darkest parts of Erik, because she knew she could digest them. Mya *wanted* to digest them, to steep in them and make them hers, because they called to something in her that could understand them, something that knew them.

Erik met her eyes, reading her desire to create more bonds between them. He was the entry to her exit, the positive to her negative, and she was his. He tightened his grip on her shoulder, then relaxed as if to let her slip away from him should she need to.

She did not. The thought of leaving him would never enter her mind.

"They did not get far from where they attacked you. Walter"—Erik said his name as if it was worse than the Black Plague—"was unconscious, and they were carrying him back to one of their estates."

Erik spun his fingers above the hearth. The fire built, responding to the anger and edge in his tone. "I broke their limbs so they could not walk, then I dragged them into the woods. There I tortured them for information. They had attacked and raped several other women, so I broke a bone for each of them. Then I carved their flesh and tore chunks out of it, making sure not to hit vital organs or veins. I left them to bleed to death, starve, or be eaten—whichever came first. Once they died, I broke their carcasses down and left them to the wolves. What they did not devour, I burned to ash.

"I found the women they attacked and have offered them employment, as well as a guard that will travel with them should they decide to take the position. That, unfortunately, was the best that could be done."

Fury rolled off Erik in waves, and Mya knew he wished he could do more. She squeezed his waist.

"They got what they deserved, and you have done

well. I am sure those women will accept your offer. Perhaps they will be able to build a better life for themselves than what they had previously been afforded."

Erik nodded, his gaze on the fire as he said, "You are taking all of this rather well."

She turned to him. "Did you think your brutality would scare me?"

"Not scare you, but give you pause."

"As I said earlier, I wanted them dead. I wanted to know how you killed them to know the depths of your rage, to know what it looks like when it is controlled. I would have not been able to think the way that you did, but perhaps with adequate training I will be able to remove myself from the situation enough to ensure I have covered all my tracks."

Mya took his hand and stepped in between him and the fire. "You are my inspiration, Erik, in many ways. You will never scare me. My trust in you has not wavered, nor will it ever."

His breath hitched. He squeezed her hand, and when he spoke his voice was lower, deeper. "We should go to bed."

She nodded and gave him a small smile as she followed him to the bed. She laid on her side with Erik behind her, but she noticed that he made sure not to touch her in any way.

"Erik?"

"Yes?"

"Hold me the same way you did the other night," she whispered, as she tried to temper her nerves.

He sighed. "You may not be ... comfortable."

"I will be just fine. Come," she said as she patted the bedding draped over her hip.

Erik moved behind her until he was pressed against her back. She lifted her head for his arm, and he shifted her hair to the side. "Would you like me to braid it for you?"

A tiny smile graced her face. "No, unless it will bother you this way?"

"It never bothers me," he breathed. "I have an obsession with your hair. I like how long and wild it is." He ran his fingers through her curls, bunching and twisting them between his fingers before gently sweeping them over her shoulder.

She blushed, happy he could not see her expression as he wrapped his arm around her. Mya intertwined their fingers and pushed back closer to him, wanting to eliminate any space between them. She bent her knees, and he followed the movement, tucking his legs behind her, but as he moved, she felt something hard against her buttocks. She wiggled, trying to understand what it was, when suddenly Erik gripped her hips.

"Stop moving," he said, his tone a warning.

"But what is that?"

"The reason why I said you would be uncomfortable."

"I do not understand." She tried to move back again, to feel the hardness once more, but he held her still.

"I have an erection, Mya."

Her eyes widened and her mouth dropped into an 'O' before she stammered, "Oh, but, well … why? W-We have not done anything."

He laughed, each breath hot on her neck. "We do not have to do anything. Being near you is enough. It will settle on its own."

His words, his body against hers, and the knowledge that her presence was enough to rile him did something to her. Her nipples became erect, her throat dry, and she had to force herself to swallow multiple times. Then she licked her lips and whispered, "Should I assist you?"

The arm under her head tensed, her only forewarning before he grabbed her by her throat and gripped her hips tight enough that it would have left a bruise if she were human. The move only served to excite her more. She bit her lip, trying to stop the moan before it left her, but he heard it, just as she knew he felt her tilt her head back further to offer him more of her throat.

"I told you not to test me further, Mya. This is the last time I will warn you," he growled, his lips touching her ear with every word. Then he relaxed and withdrew his hand from around her neck, leaving her whimpering at the loss.

"Sleep," he ordered.

She did not think she would be able to, but after

several minutes of feeling the rise and fall of his chest and the rhythm of his heartbeat behind her, she fell into a deep, peaceful rest.

—————

When Mya awoke, her head was on Erik's chest. Her arm rested on his stomach, and their legs were intertwined. She lifted her head to watch him as he slept, then gently ran her fingers through his hair. She took in his features, looked over his light golden, almost silver eyebrows, the long pale eyelashes that surrounded the orbs she loved to gaze into, his straight nose that narrowed at the bridge before widening in a perfect triangle at his nostrils. She scanned the hairs of his beard, itched to scratch them with her fingernails—

"Are you finished staring at me?"

She nearly jumped out of her skin when her eyes caught his. "I thought you were asleep."

"I was until you woke up." His large hand spread along her back as he stretched, but he made no effort to move away from her. "Did you sleep well?"

She nodded and smiled shyly. "Very. I believe that may have been the best sleep I have ever had."

He met her smile with one of his own. "I am honored to hear that."

Mya hesitated, then decided to take advantage of their position. She gently ran her fingertips through his beard, earning herself a soft moan from him. She did it again, gently scratching the area.

"How did you sleep?" she asked.

"Incredibly well, thanks to you." His eyes closed as she continued to scratch him, and a soft, satisfied rumbling noise started in his chest.

She loved the sound, loved being able to touch him freely like this, so close, so intimately. She wanted this to happen again, every night, forever, and she could not stop herself from speaking her wish out loud. "Perhaps we could do this again?"

He grabbed hold of her wrist and kissed her hand, but the look in his eyes was pained, forlorn. "You know we cannot," he said quietly.

She averted her eyes from his, so he touched her cheek. "Mya…"

A strength borne out of frustration of the unfairness of it all blossomed inside her, and she turned back to him, eyes set ablaze. "I heard what you said. I listened to your story. I understand what you feel, even though your strength of character amazes me."

He opened his mouth to speak, but she refused to hear him deny her.

"Erik, I love you. I have always loved you in the way a woman loves a man."

His mouth dropped open and his eyes widened in surprise. At the look of utter shock on his face at her outburst, she finally realized that Erik did not believe he was capable of love. She was not fighting for them; she was fighting against his guilt.

"I love you," she said again. "In my sea of anger and hatred, the one thing that my heart has never wavered on is you. The only thing I see is you. You are the greatest source of good in my life. My angel, my hero, my protector, my confidant. But you are so much more than that to me."

She touched his lips softly, tracing them with her fingertips. "I know you do not see yourself that way. I know you may believe that my feelings were borne from what you have given me. You have provided for me, kept me fed, warm, and secure. You saved my life. I will not lie to you and say that is not where my love first stemmed from. It did."

She took a deep breath and let it rush out of her, carrying away her fears, her insecurities. She knew he needed to hear her words as much as she needed to say them.

"But that was when I was younger, when I did not know or understand what these feelings were, nor the depths of them. I understand them now. I love you for the man that you are, the vampire you are, for the good-ness and darkness that is in you. I ponder you. I am curious of you. You uplift and inspire me. I want to be a better person, not only for myself but to one day be a partner to you."

She bit her lip, swallowing the deep wave of emotions between them. "You are what I want in a husband. You are who I see my future with, and I will not let anything, even you, ruin that image unless I am truly not what you desire."

His eyes were luminous, bold and immaculate as they stared into hers like they could reach the deepest depths of her soul. His chest rose and fell so quickly under her, that his body trembled with each breath. Then his hand cupped her cheek, his palm warm and firm.

"You are everything I desire, *fagr skjaldmær min.* You are everything I dream of so frequently, so often, in fact, that it ruins me when I wake and you are not next to me. My existence revolves around you. My heart beats solely for you. My thoughts are yours. My body is yours. My soul yearns to be tied to yours so strongly that I can hardly bear a moment without you. You are here," he said, pointing to his heart, "at the very core, the essence of my being. You are the air I breathe."

Words failed her under his confession. Her body seemed to fall away until she was nothing more than a heart that hung onto his every word.

"My love for you knows no bounds, no cliffs, no limits. It is immeasurable, endless, and it is because of that love for you that I must protect you."

Mya shook her head, but Erik cupped her cheeks, wiped the tears that had dampened them, and held her to him. "If anything were to ever happen to you, I would never forgive myself. *That* would be my greatest sin. Your safety is of the utmost importance to me, and that includes the safety of your heart, *fagr skjaldmær min.* Too much stands in our way for me to take you the way I dream of, to court you, to ask for your hand in marriage. I wish, oh how I wish it was different, Mya. I so desperately want to be selfish with you."

"Then be selfish with me!" She gripped his wrists, his arms, anything to keep him close, to keep him from slipping away. "Tell me what you need, what *we* need to do to finally obtain that reality."

His fingers rubbed at her temples, then slipped into her hair. "Mya..." he began, as if to tell her it was impossible to believe in such a fate. But then he sighed. "I lost myself to my blood lust. I must be vigilant. I must be ruthless and unyielding in my watch over you and your family."

"But for how long?" she lamented.

"Three hundred years," he said, dropping his eyes from hers as she gasped. "Between a vampire's two hundredth to three hundredth year, they change. Blood lust becomes less catastrophic on the mind. It is easier to control. Cravings for blood become less, allowing the vampire to go longer between feedings, and they receive an ability. I had reached my three hundredth year when I turned your brother. Had I not, I might have killed him when I turned him."

Erik traced her cheek with his thumb in a featherlight caress. "I could never ask you to wait that long, not for me. Perhaps you will find someone else, someone less—"

Anger blazed within her. "Do you truly believe my feelings for you are so fickle that they would fade? That I could ever look at another man the same way I look at you?"

"Mya—"

"Are your feelings for me so little that they could be so easily erased by something as simple as time?"

His eyes narrowed. "Of course not."

"Then do not insult me in such a manner! If you need me to wait three hundred, four hundred, one thousand years for you, Erik, I will do it."

"But that is not fair to you!"

She stroked his beard as she spoke to him softly. "That is where you are mistaken, my love. What is not fair to me, is asking me to spend a single day without you."

He pulled her to him and rested his forehead against her own as they shared the same breath. Yet even with their closeness, her body still trembled, terrified of his rejection. Erik held her, gathered her closer, and she clung to him and let his warmth seep into her bones, her very soul, fighting for any thread of connection they could form to the future they both wanted.

Then, Erik whispered to her, "We will meet here."

She lifted her head from his. "I do not understand."

"I told you I have to protect you, and right now you are so scared I will continue to fight against us that you are trembling like a leaf in the wind." He tucked her hair behind her ear. "I do not want to fight us, *fagr skjaldmær min,* and if it makes you feel this way then I simply cannot."

Her eyes widened in understanding. "Then you mean—"

"You asked me to train you, and I will. Here. After that training, should you allow me, I will court you. I cannot do so publicly," he warned. "England is in a state of unrest from the plague, and nations are still threatening war. We do not know when we may meet another immortal, and if they will be a friend or foe. If they become our enemy, you are the first person they will come after. For your safety, our courtship must stay a secret. But..." He sighed and held her tightly. "May the gods strike me down, I cannot continue to resist you."

Mya threw her arms around him and held him with all her strength as she buried her head in his neck.

"I do not deserve you, Mya. That will never change, but I will spend my entire life trying to be worthy of you."

They met in the middle, lips brushing against one another in a kiss that was both passionate and caring, wild and gentle. It was everything, and in it Mya found a sense of completion.

————

Erik kissed her head. "We should head back now. You need to eat."

Mya snuggled closer to him. "I have been drinking extra blood over the last few days, I am fine."

He made a humming noise and she rose from his chest. "Do you need to feed?" she asked.

"No, I still have a week and a half before I will need to."

An idea sparked in her head. She blushed, and although her skin did not pinken, Erik noticed her shyness and touched her cheek. "What are you thinking of?"

Her eyes flickered to his and she bit her lip softly before saying, "Would you like to?"

"What?"

"Feed. From me?" Mya gathered her hair, brushing it to the side to show him her neck.

It was a magnificent thing to see the way she affected him. He had spent so much time hiding it before, but his body was open to her now. His chest rumbled from the shuddered breath he took, and his eyes grew dark. Erik traced her cheek, then slid the backs of his fingers over the side of her exposed neck, making her shiver.

"What an enticing offer. So tempting. So delicious."

His voice grew breathless, and it caused her to pant as if he was stealing the breath from her very body. He kissed her neck, and a bolt of electricity shot straight down to her core. He did it again, trailing his lips over her skin. Each touch unleashed another tendril of desire in her.

"I want to bite you, *fagr skjaldmær min.* I cannot get the taste of you out of my head."

He hummed along her skin and the vibration made her moan. "But I will not bite you here."

"Why?" she asked, her voice husky and wanton.

"Because if I bite you here"—he nibbled her neck, and she jerked forward in surprise as another moan left her lips—"then I will spend the next two days thrusting into you like a possessed man. I will fill you with so much of my seed that you will never be able to rid yourself of me."

Her eyes fluttered closed at the picture of how he would feel inside her. Her hips rocked against his once more and she rubbed herself along his growing erection.

Erik smiled. "You would like that, I see."

Unable to speak, she bit her lip and nodded.

He chuckled. "I will bite you here, instead." He touched the space between her neck and shoulder. "That way I will let you leave this bed, but only after I give you pleasure."

Mya wrapped her arms around him, and Erik drew her close. He grabbed hold of her hips and rolled them once, twice, then widened his legs, forcing her to widen her own and sink down onto his erection. He lifted his hips, and they ground against one another.

Erik captured her lips, her moan, kissing her and taking her over completely, fanning the flames between them as he owned her with his teeth and tongue. She was breathless, shameless, whimpering when he pulled away, surrendering herself to him when he coaxed her mouth open, grinding on him, moving with him, begging for more.

Then he kissed her chin and dragged his lips and tongue down her neck to lave at her clavicle, making the hairs on her body stand on end as every nerve came alive at his touch. Still, he moved her hips, and her core grew wetter. She knew he could smell her desire—she could smell it herself—and she pulsed against him, her entrance throbbing. Mya wished he would slide inside of her, do anything to temper the delirious ache.

"I know," he whispered against her skin.

Mya wondered if she had spoken aloud, or if he knew because he felt it too. He was so hard under her, and at his words he pulled her closer and pushed against the bundle of nerves right above her pulsing lips.

Mya cried out as pleasure snaked through her, making her arch her back. He moved against the same spot, and she moaned again, the sound so lewd and loud.

Erik twitched beneath her. "Beautiful," he purred. "Such a beautiful sound. Cry for me again, *fagr skjaldmær min.* Let me hear what I do to you. Tell me how it feels."

"I—"

He ripped the tunic at her shoulder, and then his teeth pierced her flesh and she screamed his name.

Mya thought she would know what to expect when Erik bit her, but she was unprepared for the sudden, overwhelming surge of pleasure. The small tinge of pain only added to it, and she felt as if she were flying. With each gulp of blood he swallowed, with each brush against her, he sent her higher and higher.

Erik wrapped his hand around her throat and squeezed. The sensation exhilarated her, and she became needy, desperate for the next taste of her high. Mya tore at his tunic, needing to feel his skin, and when she did she clawed at his back. He moaned, and the sound turned her feral, animalistic. Their movements changed, tinges of violence in their pumping as they ground harder, faster.

Then Erik pulled back, and the sight of his lips coated in her blood made her shiver.

He snaked his hand into her hair and pulled her to him until they were only a breath apart. His eyes blazed into hers, glowing silver and tinged with red at the edges, captivating and magnificent.

Her breath caught in her lungs, and she felt as though she were soaring through the cloud. Suddenly she feared falling, so overwhelmed by pleasure and the tears that began to blur her vision. She clung to him, and he grabbed hold of her, squeezing her behind.

"Erik, it-it is so … so much. I—" She moaned, but when he rubbed along the spot once more, she cried his name, all other words forgotten.

"Do not be scared, *fagr skjaldmær min.* This is exactly how it should be. Succumb to it. Break for me."

His fingers pressed into her skin as he grasped her tightly, as if he were both commanding her and traveling along this new world with her. Mya knew she was not alone, that Erik could still protect her and keep her safe even in something she did not know.

Then he whispered, "I am right here with you."

At his words she shattered into a million pieces. Her back arched of its own accord, and her legs tightened around his hips while she bucked and thrashed and ground against him, ascending to some higher plane while begging for more. He was the only thing she knew, her anchor, her savior and torturer, and she screamed his name as the feeling flew through her body.

"So glorious," he said, his voice so incredibly deep as he moaned for her. "Your release is such perfection, *fagr skjaldmær min.* I must see it again."

The praise lit a new fire in her, and even though she could barely breathe, she watched him, took in his furrowed brow, the tension on his face, the way he seemed to be losing all control. The elation, the desire, the need to have him pumping through her veins took over and her canines extended.

"Bite me," he ordered, and she did.

The first taste of him was like the legends of ambrosia—pure goodness, pure sin—and the way he threw his head back and surrendered to her gave her a type of power that became an instant addiction.

He cradled her head to his shoulder as she took long, deep gulps, sucking and drinking him in. She was lost in the taste, the feel of him, the sounds that poured from within his throat.

He leaned forward, and Mya adjusted, planting her feet on the bed, spreading her legs open wider, wantonly. The position helped her spread her lips and she moved with Erik, dragging herself against his erection. He was so hard, so long and thick for her that even through the material of their clothes the tip of him rubbed along her opening.

Mya placed her hands on his thighs to lean back and offer herself to him in that way, in any way, in *every* way, but Erik pushed her onto her back, so she wrapped her arms around him, and together they fell back onto the bed. She pulled away from his shoulder and met the crazed look in his eyes with one of her own.

There was no room for words when Erik captured her lips. She squeezed the back of his neck, his shoulders, while he pulled and bunched the material of the tunic above her waist. Then he pressed himself against her once more, and Mya arched her back in response. Her hips came off the bed only to be pressed back down by his own. He weighed her down with his body, and she savored the feel of him.

Their kiss was a battlefield filled with gasps and moans. Erik grabbed both of her wrists and pinned them above her head, and Mya grabbed hold of anything that she could, his thumb, his index finger, squeezing them as he continued to grind against her.

They moved so franticly that the bed rocked back and forth against the wall. Erik spread her legs wider, pushing against her harder, his erection slipping between her folds. The feel of him behind the material drove her wild.

"You are so wet for me," he growled.

"Yes," she hissed, lifting her hips against his again.

He grabbed her, tilted her body to fit his in the way he wanted, and continued to rock against her. "Break for me again, *fagr skjaldmær min. Break with* me. Let me see you in ecstasy."

Her eyes closed as pleasure took over. It traveled from her head down to her toes, and she curled them as wave after wave hit her. The waves came closer and closer together, her mind in the throes of ecstasy as a large crescendo flowed through her body. She exploded, crying out, and Erik moved once, twice, before he joined her with his own roar of pleasure.

CHAPTER 8

Mya and Erik returned home with blissful smiles on their faces, until they found Gregori waiting for them. Gregori's eyes roamed over her, noting the lack of her dress and how it had been replaced by Erik's tunic. Judging by his expression, he would give them approximately one minute to formulate an explanation or else he would pummel Erik, whether he was an older and thus more powerful vampire or not.

Together they constructed a lie, explaining that her dress had been ruined on her way to the cabin, and Mya sent Erik on his way. She and Gregori had made a deal after all, and the idea of not keeping her promise––especially after lying to him––filled her with guilt. He deserved better.

Telling her brother of her assault was both embarrassing and relieving. He did not judge her or criticize her or think she was weak. Rather, he understood, hugged her, and even through bared teeth he spoke the words that she did not realize she needed to hear.

"I am so proud of you."

Mya had always looked up to her brother, and it seemed she still sought his approval after all these years.

In an effort to be open and vulnerable with him, she told him she would be training with Erik from now on. Her brother believed it was a good idea, even though he made her promise to alert him if she ever believed she was in danger, instead of trying to handle the situation on her own.

Her training lessons with Erik started later that day. Even though she had watched Erik train her brother and cousin for years, it had not prepared her in any way for her own training. He did not take pity on her just because she was a woman, nor because he loved her, something that made her respect and admiration for him grow that much stronger. Over time he taught her how to breathe to execute certain attacks, and how to block incoming ones. Mya was a little over thirty centimeters shorter than Erik, so he taught her how to use her size and lithe form to her advantage. He explained how to take attacks and what they felt like to make sure she would not be surprised, and then he taught her weaponry.

Months of training turned into years. True to his word, after they had cleaned and changed, Erik courted her. He took her on picnics and long walks through the forest. He brought her to a waterfall and taught her how to hunt animals and fish. For the first time in a long time, Mya was happy. Their relationship might have been a secret she kept from her family, but Erik was her joy. She swore to herself that she would always make the most of her moments with him, especially once everything began to change.

Their time of living in England had come to an end. Immortals needed to move often to avoid questions as to why they never seemed to age once they reached adulthood, and if they stayed much longer people would begin to grow suspicious. As such, Erik contacted his friend Miriam who was only too happy to assist them in relocating to France and become their host for a few years.

Mya should have been overjoyed at the chance to leave England, but the thought barely crossed her mind. Instead, she spent far too long being jealous of Erik's friend. Miriam was someone who had been in Erik's life longer than Mya had, someone who had been able to help him, who knew him in a way Mya did not.

And she hated it.

She knew it was foolish. Mya wanted Erik to have support from another immortal, someone he could lean on and share his responsibilities with, but she did not want it to be with another woman, someone he had known for hundreds of years longer than he had known her.

Mya tried to ignore her feelings. When that did not

work, she tried to talk herself through them. When that proved fruitless too, she hid them all together. She believed she had been doing an excellent job in that regard, until Erik cornered her by her bedroom door to ask her why she was sulking.

She narrowed her eyes. "I am not sulking."

He turned her to face him and wrapped his arms around her waist. "Ah, we are still playing this game. Pouting then? Do you even have a word for the look on your face?"

Mya rolled her eyes and tried to ignore the thrill of excitement that coursed through her body at his nearness.

"Careful, *fagr skjaldmær min*. The last time you rolled your eyes at me, you were screaming my name."

She gasped and her eyes nearly bulged out of her skull. "Erik! Hush!"

He grinned. "I am simply trying to be helpful. Are you pouting because you would like a repeat performance? I would be happy to give it to you right now."

Mya put her finger to his lips and angrily whispered to him, "Someone will hear you!"

His eyes twinkled with mischief. "No, someone will hear *you*. I have often wondered how loud I could make you scream. I guess now is the time to find out." He bent his head near hers. At the rush of her breath, his grin turned into a full smirk.

"Erik!" she whisper-shouted, but he kept coming closer and closer until his lips brushed hers.

"Tell me," he said, the low timber of his voice making her sigh. Her body heated and she relaxed into him. Mya tilted her head up to meet his lips, but he still would not kiss her, only brush his lips against her own teasingly, seductively.

"Erik," she pleaded.

"Tell me," he said again as his hands followed the curves of her body.

He won what was left of her common sense. The spell was cast, and she abandoned everything to him, including the truth. "I am jealous of Miriam."

Erik pulled back at her words. "Why would you be jealous of her?"

Possibly because I am jealous of everyone who entered your life before me.

She sighed and dropped her chin to avoid his eyes. "She has been with you for a long time. I do not know your relationship—"

"There is not one."

She opened her mouth to interject, but he grabbed her chin and tilted her head up to his, making her meet his eyes. "There is nothing more than friendship between us."

"But—"

"Mya, I had not touched a woman *willingly* until you. Miriam and I are only friends. In truth, she would be more interested in you than me, or any man for that matter."

Mya raised her eyebrow and cocked her head to the side. "I do not understand."

Erik chuckled and ran his thumb across her cheek before tucking her hair behind her ear. "She is only interested in bedding women, my love. Men do nothing for her, and if she is ever linked to a man then she is using them for her own gain."

Mya's jaw dropped. Erik laughed at her, causing her cheeks to grow warm. His eyes still twinkled as he said, "I apologize if I did not explain that correctly to you before, but I will make it clear to you now. There is no one--no woman, man, child, or animal--that I have cared for or will care for in the same way I care for you. You are, and will always have, my heart."

She made a soft whimper as his lips met hers. "I apologize," she said in between their kisses.

"No need," he murmured as he opened the bedroom door behind her and moved her over the threshold. Kicking the door shut, he guided her backward to her bed. "If you mentioned any man with fondness in your voice, I would have felt the same as you. I would have tried to kill him too."

Mya giggled as they tumbled onto the mattress together. Erik spread her legs and fit his hips against her, circling, grinding, drawing a moan from her with the movement she had come to love so much.

"Now, I believe it is time to make you scream, *fagr skjaldmær min.*"

———

Something was wrong.

One moment they were packing for the start of their new life in France with Miriam, and the next Erik had been called away by a messenger. At first, Mya figured it was nothing more than a small nuance Erik would need to resolve due to his position as lord. It was a common thing, and with the war brewing between England and France, a village needing supplies or townsfolk rioting in the streets would not be surprising.

But he had been gone for far too long.

Mya packed away her last few belongings and set off to find him. Turning into his chambers, she found him pacing. Her heart fluttered knowing he was safe, but the energy pulsating from him twisted her gut.

"What has happened?" she asked.

He sighed when he saw her, then drummed his fingers along the wooden table. "Our path has been cut off by the war."

Mya's eyes widened. "What does that mean? Can we take another path, or will we be unable to leave?"

"We have to go now." Erik began to pace once again. "It is imperative that we leave during the confusion of the battles between England and France. That will be the excuse used for our supposed deaths and why no one will be able to find our bodies. We cannot wait any longer. If the two countries reach another treaty, we may be at peace for too long, and as lord my disappearance, especially with you and your family, will seem suspicious. King Edward would likely hire spies to investigate, and we cannot let them find us. It must be this way," he said, as he ran his hand roughly through his hair.

Mya cocked her hip on the side of a table and folded her hands in her lap. "If that is our only option, then it is exactly what we must do."

"We will be walking through a battlefield, Mya," he said, arms flinging around his body.

"And," she began as she took her hands in his, "we will be just fine."

He sighed at her touch and intertwined his fingers with her own. His shoulders dropped as some of his worry seemed to leave him. "I do not know how you can say that."

She smiled. That such a strong, protective man who could act so easily, so methodically in the heat of the moment, who planned and took care of so many, could doubt what he had taught those around them never failed to surprise her. While Erik had many who trusted him, he still could not trust himself.

"I can say that, my love, because I have spent the majority of my life around you, and you have been training me and my family for years."

"But—"

She shook her head. "I know you are concerned that our blood lust will get the better of us, especially if we are caught in the crosshairs of the battle and are forced to fight. I understand that concern. It is a valid one, but you are forgetting one small thing."

She held her hand to his face, fingers nearly meeting one another to show the measurement. He sighed again at the action, but a small smile ghosted his lips and Mya swore the room brightened.

"And what did I forget, *fagr skjaldmœr min?*"

"You. We will not be alone. We will have each other and you."

He opened his mouth to speak but she held a finger to his lips to shush him. "I do not say that to mean we should rely on you, nor are we your responsibility. While we may be young vampires, we are old enough to do better. *You* have taught us to do better, to stay in control."

Mya patted his chest softly and smoothed the fabric of his tunic. Erik made a small *hmm* of pleasure as he gathered her closer.

"I know you will always feel that we are your responsibility, and you will always be there for us to rely on should we need it. But you are a leader, my love. Trust us to know our limits and to share when we feel ourselves reaching them. Lead us, and we will follow you. We are not alone," she said again, "and neither are you."

He dropped a kiss on her forehead as he held her head to his chest. "When did you become so wise?"

She giggled and tightened her hold around him. "I believe I may have learned that from you too."

———

Erik was right.

The first sign of the war were the empty villages, where the only life seemed to be the crows and small animals scavenging the roads. It appeared that everyone had left in a hurry; furniture lay tossed outside homes, rotting food turning to mush underfoot. At least, Mya hoped, the townspeople had made it to safety.

The next village had not been so lucky. Bodies lay in the roads, their blood lining the streets and seeping into the soil. Erik tried to keep her from witnessing the massacre, but she refused to hide behind their carriage blinds. Mya needed to see the carnage, to be able to stomach that someone once filled with life could now be nothing more than a corpse strewn and discarded like trash. These were the terrors of war, and she knew it would only get worse; she needed to use what she could to prepare for what was to come.

Eventually they could no longer continue by carriage, the roads blocked by bodies of humans and animals alike. They had not traveled as far as Erik had wanted them to, but they had no other choice.

As Mya, Erik, Gregori, and Lucas exited the carriage, they each took a small bag which contained spare sets of clothes, any items that held sentimental value to them, and containers of blood and water. They opened the rest of their luggage and tossed it around the carriage to look like a robbery. Then Erik, Gregori, and

Lucas walked back to the closest village to find dead men who would play them in their false tale.

Mya took this time to change. Women were not allowed on the battlefield; her mere image would be enough of an oddity and she would be remembered by anyone who survived. She dressed in Erik's tunic and a pair of Lucas's trousers. Both were far too big for her, so she tucked the tunic into the trousers and tied a piece of fabric around both to keep them from falling. Then she tied her hair at her nape, braided the length, and tucked it into the back of the tunic. She knew the disguise would not stand up to much scrutiny, but her vampire speed would keep anyone from seeing the truth.

When she finished, Mya looked at the carriage one last time. She felt the bag at her hip and the difference of the clothes that now covered her body, and she was hit by the reality of what would soon occur.

She was not upset about faking her death, nor leaving England, but she had made several of her first, most important memories there: the first time she had felt desire for Erik, their first kiss, their first touch, the first time she had felt free. He, rather than the country, was at the epicenter of so many of her happy memories, yet for all the things she hated about England, she was familiar with it. She knew where the apothecary was. She knew how to get medicine. She had a dedicated space for her experiments, and she knew where to go and what streets to take to access the poor and give them the medicine they had no other means of being able to afford.

Mya also knew she was not the only one who felt this way. Erik had changed so many lives in his reign as lord. He had done so much good, and who was to say the person who fell in line behind him would do the same? What about Gregori? Lucas? What about their memories and hopes and dreams? Leaving England, changing their names, falsifying their deaths--there would be no way to undo any of those decisions.

France would be new: new roads, society, culture, language, people, places. New expectations. There would be so much to learn and experience. Lucas was good at seeing that, at simply enjoying the spectacle of hope, of what was new and fun and spontaneous. He appreciated adventure, while Mya feared it.

But what other choice did they have?

The answer was clear when she watched the men reappear with a body on each shoulder.

They placed each body in the carriage, toppled it over, then in one final act, Erik set the carriage on fire.

They watched it burn together, each caught in their own thoughts, until the footsteps of their armies grew closer. With a sigh they left and traveled through the woods to the open battlefield.

The gunshots were deafening, sending a ringing pain through Mya's ears. She shook her head and remembered this was why Erik had told her they could not use guns. One moment of weakness could give someone—even a human—enough leeway to kill an immortal. All it took was a brain injury, and the new, experimental weaponry the armies were using, were accurate enough now to destroy the complex organ.

Erik ran through the rules once more as they waited in the tree line: Focus on killing the gunmen first, preferably from behind to eliminate risks. Use swords or knives to appear human, instead of relying on your strength. If at any point you feel the need to drink blood, drain the blood in the bags first.

They nodded and stood together, waiting for his signal. Mya knew the moment they leapt forward, everything would change. Whether or not they wanted it to, they were about to make history, to aid England in winning a war regardless of whether they truly believed they deserved to, only because the French army stood in their way. But for their survival, it had to be done.

Erik's fingers brushed her own as if he could feel the grimness in her, and she turned her hand into his and gave it a small squeeze. When they released, he took one breath, then whispered the command.

"Go."

They sped through the air as they fanned out along the field. Mya reached her first man. His gun was leveled at a soldier, and before he took his next breath, she cut off his head. His body crumpled to the ground as life left him so quickly, so effortlessly. The whole ordeal was over in a second, and it was then she realized she was no different than him.

For just a moment she wondered if he had a family, someone he was fighting for just as she was. But then, she shook her head, regulated her breathing, and reminded herself she could not go down that road. Erik was out there. Her family was out there. She could not fall behind and she could not let this overtake her. After all, this was war, and there would always be sacrifices in war.

Mya killed another man, and another, and another until she lost count. If there was any goodness to be found in this, it was that she made sure they did not feel any pain. She tried to be merciful and killed each man quickly, without hesitation. But in her pathway of death and destruction, she did not notice the gun trained on her from the line of the trees until it was too late.

The shot was so loud it made her head spin, but she forced herself to focus. The bullet would hurt when it hit her shoulder, but she would heal quickly. Then she would be sure to kill that man and anyone else she found hidden away before they could possibly hurt her family.

She prepared for the impact—closed her eyes, took a deep breath to ready herself for the pain—but it did not come. Instead of the expected bullet, she felt a shadow fall over her, and when she looked up, she saw Erik.

He stood in front of her, his back to her, and for a

split second she thought he had taken the bullet in her place. Panic gripped her chest. She reached out for him, only to hear him roar. The sound, like a murderous beast, was louder than any gunshot, any scream, any cry of pain.

The temperature rose around them. Mya called to Erik, but her voice was not enough to break him from his spell. She understood the only thing that would do so was the blood of the man who had shot at her, and so she waited behind Erik and allowed him to take vengeance on her behalf.

Flames rippled out of his body, four lines that poured over the battlefield, melting the flesh of the fallen and setting those in its path on fire. The scent of their charred bodies coated the air as their screams echoed around them.

Erik roared again and the flames lifted, floating in the sky before combining. They stilled for a second, then sped toward the man in the trees. The flames burned so hot, so brightly, they vaporized him in an instant.

Erik's hand twitched as he widened the fire, spreading it further and further, burning the trees, the space around them. More men screamed, and their voices were joined by more and more, and more until...

Mya touched Erik's back, molded herself to it, and whispered, "I am right here. You saved me. You protected me. You can stop now."

His powers calmed, but the damage was done. The flames spread along the forest naturally now, burning brush and trees.

"No one harms you, ever," Erik said. His voice was so deep, so dark and commanding that it shook her to her core, then he turned. She felt her breath catch as she took in the blend of silver, red, and orange in his eyes. Before she could say a word, he cupped her cheek and slammed his lips against her own.

He kissed her as if they were not on a battlefield, as if they were not surrounded by death and dismay, as if the scent of his victims did not still hang in the air. His kiss was commanding, all-consuming, refusing to allow any space between them. He was her water, her air, her core, her anchor to this world. Without him she would float away. She kissed him just as hard, just as passionately, giving everything that she was and taking all of him in return.

A large crash sounded behind them, making them break apart, but Erik refused to loosen his hold from her, so she turned to face the new challenge with him.

He relaxed against her slightly as a carriage came into view. The door opened and out stepped a pale woman with long, straight black hair, and dark, almond shaped eyes. She smiled when she saw him, and Erik gave her a tiny smile in return.

"Hello, Miriam."

"It is nice to see you again, Erik. Although next time

could you try to rein in your fire? You almost damaged the carriage, and this thing cost a fortune.”

He rolled his eyes. “Only you would bring something of high value to a battlefield.”

“You will not be complaining when the expensive cushions keep your arse from being sore.”

A small hiccup of laughter left Mya’s lips, drawing Miriam’s gaze.

“Ah, you must be his—”

“Mya,” Erik interrupted. “This is Mya.”

Miriam paused, and Mya looked between the two, wondering what it was that Erik had stopped her from saying.

“It is lovely to meet you, Mya. I have heard a lot about you.”

Mya met her smile with one of her own. “And I, you.”

She tried to leave Erik’s embrace to properly greet Miriam, but Erik refused to let her go, even when her brother and cousin neared them. When Mya tried to move again, Erik growled.

“Hush,” Miriam said with a dismissive wave. “I know she is yours; I will not try to steal her from you. Now, if you are done being territorial, we have a long journey ahead of us, one which I would like to start before your fire blocks our path completely.”

Mya giggled under her breath as Erik bristled. After a few seconds he finally conceded and slipped his arms from around her. He gave her a sharp look, but she ignored him and instead took his hand. "You can be territorial later," she whispered.

A grin spread across his lips as he ushered her into the carriage where they were barraged with questions about their relationship by her family and Miriam all the way to France.

CHAPTER 9

18TH CENTURY

Mya became a new woman in France.

Miriam was a thief, a charlatan, a seductress, and Mya's self-appointed mentor. According to her, Mya only knew masculine power: how to fight, bear arms, and kill someone. But there was another type of power—feminine power—and it could be just as destructive, just as chaotic, without ever needing to break a sweat.

So, Mya learned how to sing, play the harp, perform, and command a crowd, how to be mysterious, give society a taste of her and leave them wanting more, all while still being comfortable in her own skin. She learned how to take criticisms and rework them to her advantage, how to make a mockery out of stupid men who believed she should be valued less than them for simply being a woman. She learned how to gain money, influence, power, and how to bring men, and even women, to their knees, much to Erik's dismay. He did, however, enjoy that she became bolder and braver around him, especially in the bedroom.

Mya was so fulfilled that she now saw her time in England in a new light. She had even taken to keeping a journal, filled with firsts she'd had with Erik and things she had taken for granted that she was now grateful for. Her life may not have been perfect, but it was hers to live, and every hardship she faced only served to make her a better person.

Their next move was to Spain, a gift from Erik to her and her family. While they couldn't stay in the same village Mya had been born in, they were able to see the resting places of her parents and aunt. Mya spent most of her day with them, only vacating the area to allow her brother and cousin to do the same. She told them about her life and how much it had changed, how much she wished they could have been there to see it.

From Spain they went to Italy, then Switzerland, and it was there that everything fell apart.

The witch trials had been in practice for centuries, and while they had been able to avoid them in the past, this time they could not. Not only had real, practicing witches who belonged to the Magic World—the world in between the human world and the Otherworld— been tried and convicted, but the immortals they worked with had also been killed.

Every immortal knew that they were not invincible, but there had never been such a successful slaughter on their kind. And that was not the only one; there were reports all over Europe of new, young immortals being experimented on, tortured, and killed, especially in Germany and Switzerland. Humans did not seem to know what they were, just that they seemed to be different. Old lore and legends of vampires, werewolves, faeries, elves, mermaids, and more began being whispered in the shadows, and each whisper held far too much truth for their liking.

It was those whispers that made Erik, Mya, and her family finally agree to set sail for America in the hopes that they would be able to build a new, safe life there. They knew America had been stolen from its people, but Gregori and Erik had a plan. They wanted to build a council, a government for immortals. They hoped species who had previously isolated themselves from others would be willing to join them in this new leadership and realize they could have a voice within the Otherworld. With this joining, they hoped that infighting and segregation would stop. Instead of being divided forces against the new threat, they could band together to protect one another. This union offered safety, security, a new life and escape from a torturous death.

They met with Miriam, who had purchased a ship and crew members for their voyage. They gathered their food and supplies and then set sail. During the trip, they matured as vampires and received their first abilities. Gregori gained the ability to control and manipulate energy, and with enough practice he realized that could fortify it, create anything he wanted to with his energy and then use it as a real, tangible object.

Lucas's ability was to become a shadow, something that he enjoyed using to scare the crew. Over time he learned that he could also control shadows in a similar way to Gregori's ability.

But Mya's ability was different. She received the ability to heal her injuries so fast that cuts were gone in a second, broken bones knitted together in a breath, even full appendages returned in the blink of an eye. At first, she was disappointed. She had wanted something different, something stronger, something that could protect those she loved. But then she realized the power to heal did not have to be hers alone. Through her experiments she found that her healing ability did not just work on her, but also humans. A small cut would heal in a minute, and common diseases disappeared just as quickly.

Then she shared her blood with Erik and found that his own healing ability had strengthened. It was not as strong as hers, but it was enough to make a difference. She gave her blood to her brother and cousin and felt euphoric that she could both help *and* protect others. She could save anyone she wanted to. She could be *useful* in a way no one else could be, and she could fulfill a role no one could take from her--the saving grace of her family.

———

The moment they arrived in America, their plans began.

They received official paperwork, including name changes. Gregori and Lucas were forced to shorten their names, while Miriam changed hers to Lily. From there they purchased several plots of land, including a tavern and inn close to the docks. The location was perfect. Travelers arriving in America would choose to rest at the first inn they saw: theirs. Mya would get them drunk. The alcohol would loosen their lips all while she listened and deftly steered the conversation. Then she took those details and shared them with Erik and Greg. Luke would do something similar, although he seemed to have much more fun by entertaining the women in his private rooms.

It was a simple, unsuspecting con, but it was a fruitful one that yielded valuable information. They had learned local lore and legends of different possible immortals and witch specializations that they never knew existed, murders that may be immortal related, and which immortals had arrived that may be willing to join their cause.

Mya enjoyed her role as spy. While Erik went with Greg to follow new leads and barter meetings for their new council, Mya spent her days training. She pushed her body, wanting to know what her new limitations were, but could not find any. She spent days experimenting, finding out that a single drop of blood held the ability to heal disease, but only if it came from her. She used that knowledge to infuse drinks for those that were sick, those who had made the journey because they were poor and wanted a new life for themselves. She listened to their stories and sympathized with their cause, because she too wanted a better life, somewhere she wouldn't need to hide.

Then, when Erik got back from his excursions with her brother, she spent her nights with him. She enjoyed those nights, not just because of the pleasure she experienced with him but because she could hold him in her arms. At night, they weren't a secret. At night, they were a couple. She called him hers, and he called her his, and that was enough. At night, it was enough. But once the sun rose and she watched him leave, it became ... something else.

That was why Mya worked to keep herself busy. She hoped that if she was constantly moving, constantly striving to learn something new, that her thoughts and the staggering emotions that plagued her would fall to the back of her mind. She hoped that eventually they would go away, but they didn't. Each day she spent occupying herself and each night she spent with Erik seemed to only make them worse.

When would it be enough? When would *she* be enough? Because even though three hundred years had passed and so much had changed in the world, nothing had changed between them.

Mya now had full control over her blood lust. She

had received her first ability. She was helpful and useful to their family. She had proven that she could defend herself and would never be a weakness in war. She had done all these things, everything that she believed should have been enough to make Erik finally claim her, but he had not. Apart from kissing and rubbing against her until they both orgasmed, he had never entered her or taken her the way she wanted him to. She was the secret that he kept from everyone but her family.

She knew that wasn't fair. Erik relied on her, confided in her, trusted her. He made time for her, made sure to start and end his days with her, but she couldn't go with him on his outings with her brother. No one outside of their family and Lily could know they were together. They could not even say they were in a relationship. She understood that, too, understood that the murders of immortals were increasing and no one knew why. She knew Erik and Greg were investigating those crimes to try and learn more, to make sure they could get ahead of it and keep everyone safe, but this council was still up in the air, and a chance at peace, not a guarantee. Mya worried that if it didn't work, their relationship would never progress.

Mya wanted to marry Erik. She wanted to have children with him, walk the streets freely with him in the daylight, where people, immortals, anyone and anything could see. In her opinion she would be a target even if The Council formed. She would always be seen as the weakest link of the family, even if it wasn't true, but she couldn't tell Erik that. If she did, he would--as he always had--prioritize her safety above everything else, even their happiness, and she wasn't sure how much more of that she could take.

———

The tavern's patrons were loud, talking, dancing, and laughing, their spirits high as the drinks flowed endlessly. There were no empty glasses, no wait, no fuss, just joy and easy mirth.

Mya glided behind the counter, watching as the patrons ate, played cards, or left to entertain their partners in the rooms upstairs. The tavern was full to the brim as three ships had docked safely that day, bringing large groups of eager people wanting to celebrate the end of their last voyage and the beginning of their new life.

In all honesty, Mya did not like being around people, but when they were so uninhibited, so free, she found it easier. There was no need to guess what they were thinking, what stories they were spinning or lies they were telling. They were their true selves, something Mya both admired and found easy to take advantage of to help her family's cause.

She'd already heard one tale about blood witches murdering a traveling band of thieves in the next town over—the fifth one this week—and another tale of twinkling lights in the forest that someone believed were faeries. Mya believed both stories, as she knew there was a group of faeries who had come from Europe to America after war had caused the portal to their realm to burn down.

Mya's real concern were the blood witches. The immortals that had been killed had small traces of magic on them, and several had been found with their blood drained. Most of the dead immortals were werewolves, and while the lack of blood made the killings appear to be the work of a vampire, there had not been a war between vampires and shifters for almost a full century.

After further investigation, Greg noticed that the magic signature did not seem to have a limit, like theirs or any other immortals. There was only one answer: it belonged to a witch from the Magic World. They were the only ones who with time, proper casting, spell work, experience, and resources, could grow their powers exponentially.

Then the stories of blood witches began rolling in; witches who had been enslaved by vampires. It was a terrible practice that had started in Europe and continued in America. The abuse and rage the witches had suffered, brought forth a new type of magic, one that rotted away at their souls. They used the very blood in their bodies, and that of their opponent, to fuel their magic, giving them an endless stream of power. They could shift not only their bodies but the very fabric of an immortal's mind.

Mya would've admired them if they hadn't been so dangerous. She understood their need for vengeance and felt that they were justified in killing their captors, but the innocent immortals they now hunted and murdered with glee had done nothing to warrant their death.

Still, as much of a threat as the blood witches were, their attacked served to push immortals to agree to The Council and an eventual alliance, something that had never been done before. Fear could be an excellent motivator for action, and luckily Erik and Greg knew how to wield it to their advantage.

Both men entered the tavern as if her thoughts had summoned them. Greg gave her a nod and smile which she returned. Erik did the same, although his smile was larger, warming his lingering eyes which never left her frame. Even though it was something he routinely did, she still blushed under his attention.

"Aye, wench! Another round of ale!"

Mya snarled at the intrusion. She grabbed two mugs and filled them to the brim, marched over to the demanding man, and poured both glasses directly over his head. He shouted and moved to stand, but she kicked his leg out from underneath him and used his shoulder to slam him back in his seat. The tavern fell silent as all eyes turned to Mya.

"You want ale, you go to the counter and you order

it *nicely.* Call me a wench again and I'll break this glass and use it to cut out your tongue."

His face reddened as he tried to stand again. "You b—"

Mya squeezed his clavicle until the bone snapped in two. He opened his mouth to scream, but she shoved his jaw shut. Another man moved behind her to stand, and she narrowed her eyes at him.

"Sit," she ordered.

His eyes grew wide. For a split second he looked at the man she held down, who now had tears streaming down his beet red face, then back at her. Mya could feel the fear radiating off him as he slowly sat down, palms raised in submission.

Mya straightened, her eyes glancing at each man around the table. "When I release your friend, you will help him up. Then, you will leave my tavern or else I will do the same thing to every single one of you. Nod if you understand."

They gulped, and she enjoyed the way they squirmed in their chairs. After a quick look at one another, they all nodded obediently. When she lifted her hand from the man, they propped him up between them and nearly ran out of her establishment.

She sighed as the noise of the tavern returned, the scene now all but forgotten. These were the joys that came when working with people and alcohol, but she couldn't deny the small bit of pleasure she received from having power and control over her domain.

Mya signaled to one of her ladies to clean the table, then moved back behind the counter. She busied herself with serving, all the while being mindful of the man watching her in her peripheral. He continued to study her throughout the night, and she noted that he'd only ordered one drink, which he sipped slowly.

That told Mya that he was here for another reason, and as he began to approach her on sure and stable steps, with a large gait, smirk on his face, and a twinkle in his eye, Mya could tell he wasn't someone who was accustomed to taking no for an answer.

He will be once I'm done with him.

He sidled up to the counter, where he leaned silently against the wood. Mya continued wiping down the surface and ignored him. He seemed to believe she should address him, or that his presence was more important than her tasks. That wasn't how she ran things. It didn't matter if he was one of the gods themselves; he shit just like every other person in this world. If he wanted her assistance and attention, he would need to ask for it.

He stewed for a moment before he finally tipped his hat in her direction and said, "Ma'am."

She set the glass she was cleaning down, flipped her towel over her shoulder, and nodded to his drink. "Do you need a new cup of ale or something to eat?"

"No, I'm looking for something else," he purred.

She mentally rolled her eyes but did her best to keep her tone light, friendly, and short. "If you're looking for room and board, you could try the inn down the way, we're full."

"I'm not looking for that either." He set his mug down, spread his arms out across the counter and leaned down to invade her space. "What I want is you."

Mya raised her eyebrow. "Excuse me?"

"I saw the way you handled those men. I could use a woman like you. Strong. Smart. Confident. You know how to keep people in line, and you're a fighter. I like that, especially in bed."

She had to swallow the bile that raced up her throat. "I'm sure that might be flattering to someone, but I'm not interested. Move along," she said sharply, waving her hand.

He chuckled, and the laugh grated on her nerves. "It wasn't a request. If you won't come with me willingly, I'll buy you."

Her grip tightened on the counter. "What did you just say?"

"I'll buy you. I have more than enough money, and I always get what I want." His smile broadened. "In all honesty, I was hoping you'd say no. It makes me more excited to take you by force, to break you, to tame you just like I do my mares," he said, his hand inching toward her face.

Mya reared back and hit him square in the chest. She kept her palm open to stop herself from causing any permanent damage, but he still flew across the room and into a table. It broke, and each dish on top of it shattered as it hit the floor.

Time seemed to stop as each person froze and turned to her for the second time that night.

She raised a pitcher in the air and shouted, "Who wants another drink?"

A cheer roared through the room and the festivities started up again.

Mya shook her head as she watched the man leave. Lily was right: men who acted like dogs had simply never been trained. Lucky for her, Mya not only knew how to rectify that issue, she'd become an expert in it.

CHAPTER 10

Mya smiled as Erik opened the door for her and guided her to walk closer to the buildings. He flanked her side, taking the position nearest to the street. He always ensured her safety. Forever her shield. Her vigilant protector.

He walked her to the back of the tavern in comfortable silence, then led her up the stairs to her room. The moment Mya opened the door, Erik was on her, his lips crashing against her own. She wrapped her arms and legs around him as he lifted her, then kicked the door closed behind them. He all but tossed her on the bed, then stepped away from her to take the dresser and shove it against the door, blocking it from opening.

"What are you doing?"

"You won't be able to stay quiet tonight, and I don't want anyone barging in from all the screaming."

She smiled as he neared her, sitting back on her

hands and spreading her legs wide. "You're mighty sure of yourself."

He grabbed the back of her knees and pulled her until she fell back against the bed with a huff. "Are you trying to bait me, *fagr skjaldmær min*?" he asked, his voice low.

She giggled. "Is it working?"

He smirked, and the intensity in his gaze stole her breath and flooded her with heat. "You have no idea what you just started."

She opened her mouth to goad him further, but he shut it with his lips. He laid on top of her, covering her with his body, his warmth. Mya knew she would never get used to the weight of him, never get used to the way it felt to simply hold him like this.

She ran her fingers through his hair. It had grown longer, down to his mid-back now. She loved the length, loved the way he growled into her mouth when she tugged on the strands, and loved it even more when he did the same to her. He tilted her head back until she had no choice but to surrender to him, to let him use her mouth in whatever way he saw fit, to let him plea-sure her with his tongue and teeth.

He licked her mouth, delved into its depths, making her moan and writhe against him. He nibbled and bit her lips, sucked them and her tongue, and she whim-pered as the action sent pleasure coursing through her body. Her core clenched and throbbed, begging for him to do more than kiss, touch, and squeeze. She longed for him to thrust inside her.

Erik lifted his hips from hers, and when she tried to follow, to rub against him, he surprised her by changing their position.

"Give me your back and put your legs on top of mine," he ordered, and after a moment of shock, she complied.

In the corner of her room was a full-length mirror, one she could now see them in as she sat on his lap, her back to his front. In the reflection, Erik's eyes met hers. They were so dark, the silver blending to a gray so deep it was closer to metallic black. He looked devious, hungry, like a lion ready to feast on its favorite meal, and she shivered under the intensity.

Slowly he pulled on her skirts, sliding the material up her calves, her knees, her thighs, all the while never breaking his stare. She blushed and fidgeted with a need to stop him out of embarrassment, but a deeper curiosity, the desire to see what would happen next, held her still.

Her breath caught in her throat as he gripped her thighs, squeezing her flesh. His hands were so warm against her skin, but the way he held her, digging his fingernails into her flesh as if he owned her, made her shudder.

Then he began to spread his legs, forcing her own legs to follow with his grip. She gasped at the feeling of being stretched, of her body being used as a sacrificial lamb for whatever he wanted, whatever would please him. The feeling was just as freeing and intoxicating as it was overwhelming and terrifying.

"Erik, what are you doing?" Her voice was so husky and breathless that he smirked, knowing just how much he affected her, how much she wanted him.

"Open yourself for me, *fagr skjaldmær min.* Let me see that beautiful cunt. Let me see how wet you are, how badly you *need* me."

His words fanned the flames within her and made her moan, even though he had yet to touch her. There was only him, what he wanted, and the hidden promise afterward. The anticipation was too much, and she spread her legs quickly for him.

She didn't question when he lifted his knees and forced her to do the same, leaving her legs dangling over the top and side of his. As a reward for her willingness, he wrapped his hand around her throat, tilted her chin up and claimed her lips in a searing kiss. Then he pulled her skirts to her waist, leaving her completely bare and open for him to see and touch. He licked her lips, sucked them into his mouth, then his fingers reached down and stroked the small bud of her core.

She jerked against his hand in surprise, gasping and breaking their kiss. He pushed harder against her, keeping her pinned between his hips and his hand, leaving her barely able to roll her hips against him.

"Use me," he whispered into her ear, and when he

kissed the lobe it sent chills down to her toes. "Use me for your pleasure. Go wild for me, *fagr skjaldmær min.*"

She couldn't stop herself as she undulated against his hand, but even as the pleasure sought to overwhelm her, she couldn't meet his gaze in the mirror. Erik had never touched her like this, never put his hand there. She could only imagine what she looked like in the mirror, naked from the waist down, grinding herself on his fingers.

Mya buried her head in his neck. As he rubbed her faster, her moans grew louder. Then he pinched the bundle of nerves, and she cried out as an arch of electricity traveled down her spine.

"Watch yourself in the mirror, Mya."

He was so hard behind her, so tense, and every time he spoke his voice seemed to drop another octave. It was killing her, but she couldn't obey him. She *couldn't.*

"No," she shook her head frantically. "I can't, I can't," and yet she still moaned, still rubbed against him, faster now, getting closer to her release.

"No?" He chuckled in her ear. "You are not in a position to say no to me, *fagr skjaldmær min,*" he warned, and then he pinched her again.

She cried out his name as the pain mixed with pleasure and took her higher.

"Watch," he commanded.

But she still couldn't. It would be so lewd, so wrong to see herself so wanton. And yet she wanted to listen to him, to follow his instructions. She was so caught in between those emotions that she didn't hear his snarl until it was too late.

"You *will* obey me, Mya." He grabbed hold of her throat and forced her head forward, tilting it to the side. "You wanted to play with fire. Now you will know what it's like to get burned," he growled as he sunk his teeth into her neck.

Her eyes flashed open in shock, meeting the image of their reflections. She watched helplessly as he drank from her, her hips circling and grinding against his hand. She couldn't look away at the picture of them, so lost together. Her mouth was open, and each cry he tore from her seemed to reverberate even louder in her own ears. His eyes met hers in the mirror once more and then slid down to where his fingers teased and plucked at her like an instrument crafted just for him.

Erik teased her entrance, and she came. Her release was so strong, so vibrant, that for a moment she saw nothing but colors, bursts of light so bright they blinded her from everything else. Erik held her, anchoring her with his teeth and fingers. He kept moving even after her climax ended.

All she could do was fall into him, relax into his body, and moan his name in high pitched whimpers. Tears fell from her eyes as her pleasure heightened and she became nothing more than sensations and emotions.

He released her from his bite, and she arched her

neck back, silently begging, pleading for him to drink from her again.

"Such a bad girl," he murmured in her ear, but his fingers were still touching her, coaxing her.

"Why?" Mya asked, barely able to speak around her moans. She tried to grab hold of his hand so she could focus on his words, but he only quickened the pace.

"What is our one rule, Mya?"

She couldn't think, couldn't answer him.

He nuzzled her cheek with his bearded jaw, then squeezed her breast pinching her nipple. "No man touches you, *ever*. You broke that rule, Mya, and then you disobeyed me," he snarled into her ear. "You deserve to be punished."

She shook her head frantically. "I did—"

He circled her entrance, applying just a bit of pressure as he began to enter her with the tip of his finger. She was so untried that he could barely move within her, and yet every small thrust made her shake.

"I didn't! I swear. Erik ... Erik!" she cried out as he stroked her from within.

"He had plans for you, Mya," he said, as he teased her walls and she quaked around his finger, nearing another orgasm. "That stupid bastard thought he could have you, could own you, that he could make you feel the way I can."

She shook her head, unable to speak to tell him the thought was impossible. She belonged to him, only him.

"I killed him," he hissed, and his anger and fury

only added to her pleasure. "And I wanted so badly to come to you, to touch you here, like I'm doing right now." He thumbed her bud while his finger circled and stretched her deeper. "Would you have let me touch you with his blood on my hands? Would you have enjoyed that, *fagr skjaldmær min*?"

Her answer should have been no. His words should not have made her so wet that the bed was now drenched beneath her. It should not have made her nipples harder, her breathing shallower, or her body flush with heat. It was sick. It was twisted. It was exactly what she needed. The orgasm began at the base of her spine, and she felt it travel up her body, roll into her shoulders, expand into her chest—

"Such a bad girl," he purred. "So wicked. So dirty. But I will never let another man touch you, not even his blood. You are *mine*. Every inch, every curve, every cry from your lips, every kiss, every touch, every beat of your heart belongs to *me*."

She came, exploding into a symphony of stars. She traveled along galaxies and saw the vast expanse of the universe. She couldn't stop, and her body continued to spasm as euphoria filled every cell within her.

And then he took her there five more times, his fingers so coated in her juices that he was able to thrust two in and out before he finally turned her around and ground against her until he came.

After he cleaned them, they held one another. Although Mya's entire body was relaxed, her mind was active. She'd enjoyed everything Erik had done to her, but something about his ferociousness, his desperation to remind her who she belonged to when they both knew the answer, made her concerned that something else was weighing on his mind.

She turned in his arms, knowing that he was awake as she was. Mya ran her hand over his cheek and his eyelids fluttered from her touch. He grabbed her hand and kissed it softly, causing her to sigh.

"Did something happen?" she asked.

When his eyes opened, she knew she didn't need to elaborate. He kissed her hand once more and drew her head to his chest.

"You are my heart. You are the very breath in my body, what completes my soul, and I know that you have been unhappy because of me."

"Erik—"

"Please don't," he whispered. "You have been waiting for such a long time for me. *We* have been waiting for such a long time, and it's not fair to either of us."

He cupped her cheek and tilted her head to his. "You know I want this, don't you? That I want you? I want to shout to the entire world that you are mine. I want to take you with me on trips and to events without having to make an excuse as to why you are there."

"I know," she whispered, squeezing his hand. "And I know why we can't. I just…"

"I wish it could be different too, *fagr skjaldmær min*, and I promise I am trying to make it so. That is why I keep going with your brother to these council meetings. We are so close. If tomorrow's goes well, it will be done."

Her head shot up from his chest. "Really?"

Erik smiled and kissed her forehead. "Yes, and there are so many plans I have made for us, so many surprises that I can't wait to show you. I want to be with you, and this council is going to make it happen. Please, just give me one more day."

She cupped his face. "Erik, I will always wait for you. Even if I don't like the circumstances, I will never stop waiting for you. I love you."

He kissed her so gently, so tenderly, with so much love and affection that she felt covered in it from her head to her toes. So why did she want to cry?

CHAPTER 11

Mya was anxious the entire morning. She clung to Erik the moment she woke up, and he held her just as tightly. He promised her that he would come back to her, just as he always had. He told her she had no reason to worry, and when she explained the terrible sense of dread churning in her gut, he assured her he would be safe and everything would be fine. After all, how many battles had they fought together? How many times could the universe have tried to break them apart, and yet they were still standing together?

Mya couldn't argue with that. Logically, he was correct. Time after time, they had always made it through and only grown stronger. Yet the feeling stayed.

After she kissed him goodbye, she busied herself. He told her the meeting that would confirm the formation of The Council would be at 3:00 p.m. The location was only twenty minutes away. By 4:00 p.m. he would walk through the tavern doors, and all of this would be over. She just had to wait until then.

Time moved slowly. Mya checked the tavern clock constantly, thinking an hour had passed when it had only been five minutes. Frustrated, she stopped looking at it altogether and set about doing everything she could to fill her time. She cleaned things that had already been cleaned, then helped to cook items that her staff normally assisted her with.

Finally, it reached 3:00 p.m.

Then 3:15 p.m.

3:30 p.m.

3:35 p.m.

3:45 p.m.

3:55 p.m.

The doors to the tavern swung open, and Mya rushed toward them in delight, only to find her brother. Greg ran to her, picked her up and twirled her around.

"Put me down! Put me down!" she laughed, smacking his shoulders.

"Mya, we got it! We did it! We officially have a council!" Greg said, jumping and twirling around with her, narrowly missing knocking over a table and chairs.

"I am so happy for you!"

"Be happy for all of us! Some things had to change, but this is a start, a huge leap to bringing all immortals to peace."

She hugged him tightly when he set her down, then

pinched his cheeks. "You worked so hard on this! I'm so proud of you."

The smile on his face was one of pure glee. "I couldn't have done it on my own."

Mya looked around the tavern for Erik, but she didn't see him. "Where is Erik?"

"He said he had to get something and would be back a little bit later."

Panic raced throughout her body as the sense of dread returned. It was stronger now, and she doubled over, clenching her stomach.

Greg grabbed her. "Mya? Mya? What's wrong?"

"Where's Erik?"

"I don't know—"

"We have to find him! We have to find him! *Now!*" She pulled away from her brother, but he pulled her back.

"Mya, what's happening? Do you know something?"

"Something's wrong! Just please. I need to find him!" she screamed.

"I'll get Luke and go east. You go west. We'll search for an hour, then meet back here. Yes?"

She nodded and they dashed out the door. She only hoped she could find Erik in time.

———

Mya had only been searching for thirty minutes before she felt it. She didn't know what it was and couldn't describe it as anything other than a feeling. It was as if the dread has suddenly grown stronger, and out of some sick, morbid curiosity, she had to follow where it led.

She paused at an alleyway. At first couldn't understand why she had, until she heard the noise again. Beneath the sound of horses, carriage wheels, and people going about their daily activities, she'd heard moaning and grunting. She'd ignored the sounds at first —many women had to sell their bodies to eat, gather shelter, and make a name and status for themselves and their families here—but this time she'd heard the male voice, and the sound was *startlingly* familiar.

Mya followed the noise down two more streets. Then she stopped, and she felt the ground fall from under her.

It was Erik. His back was toward her, but Mya knew the width of those shoulders, the strength in those arms, the narrowness in those hips ... hips that had a pair of ankles crossed behind them as he thrusted into another woman.

The woman threw her head back in glee, and Erik groaned, the same noise, the *exact same one* he'd made with her last night. Erik wasn't even drinking from this woman. He was simply enjoying her, fucking her against the wall with the wild abandon that Mya had always wanted, craved, *desired*.

Why?

Why was this happening?

How did everything go wrong?

Why this woman?

What had she done to make him stray from her?

Just last night he had promised to stay with her forever, promised that they would be together after he secured The Council, and now he was screwing another woman against a wall.

None of it made sense.

Something clawed in Mya's gut, and a feeling flickered in her heart. Something about this was all wrong. She took a deep breath and the realization hit her. From here, she could breathe in Erik's scent, but it wasn't right. This ... *thing* didn't smell like Erik, not like his signature scent of pine, ash, smoke and cinnamon. Instead, it smelled faintly of grease, blood, and a large dose of salt.

That's not Erik! It's not Erik!

And then a chill flew down her spine. This wasn't a case of mistaken identity. Someone had done this on purpose. They *wanted* her to think this was Erik, and that made every part of her body burn with rage.

Mya stormed up to the couple, grabbed the impostor by his hair and tugged him off the woman. She threw the man against the wall, and before either of the couple could blink, she had her hand around the man's throat.

His silver eyes grew wide, and for a second, just one second, she wavered. They looked so much like Erik's, down to every sparkle and line that made his eyes uniquely his. They were a perfect replica. But that's all they were, a replica.

Mya tightened her grip on the man's throat and turned to look at the woman. "I'd recommend you leave. *Now.*"

The woman stared at Mya in a mixture of shock and horror before she scrambled to her feet and stumbled out the alley.

Mya turned back to the man and found him smiling. "What's the matter, *lover?*"

She pulled him back and pushed him into the wall again with so much force his body left an indent in the brick. "Do *not* call me that. You are not *him,*" she hissed.

He smirked. "Jealousy doesn't suit you, love."

Mya knew he was baiting her, but she refused to fall for it. "Why did you do this?"

The man's eyes narrowed, and his expression transformed to one of anger. "Because you and your kind encroached on *our* land! Do you know how many of us you've killed? How much you've taken from us? Our women? Our witches—"

His eyes widened as the last word left his mouth, but it was too late.

"What witches?"

His face relaxed and he smiled again. "That's not the question you should be asking, *immortal,*" he said, spitting the word like it was a curse.

Mya opened her mouth to speak, but then she

paused and really took in the man in front of her. He wasn't scared of her, even though he knew what she was and knew she could and *would* kill him. In fact, he looked as though he'd won something, like he knew a secret that would break her and bring her to her knees.

The realization hit her square in her chest.

If he was disguising himself as Erik, where was *her* Erik?

Her face must have given her away because the man's expression morphed into one of sick satisfaction. "You've finally figured it out then."

Her eyes narrowed. "Where is he?"

The man had the audacity to shrug. The movement should have been pathetic since he was dangling off the ground, her hand still firmly around his throat, but his nonchalance sent a shiver of fear down her back.

"I might as well tell you. My job here is done. He's at his home. I presume you know where that is, but you won't be able to save him anyway. It's too late for the both of you."

Goosebumps trailed her skin, following the wave of dread that spread throughout her body. In her rage, she tore the man's esophagus out of his body and threw it to the floor, and yet he still died with a smile on his face.

He didn't win, she told herself. *Erik would have never believed...*

But she almost had. And hadn't Erik been worried last night? Hadn't he seemed to think she was growing tired of waiting? If he had seen...

No.

No!

Mya ran as fast as she could through the alleyways to the edge of the town, then deep into the forest. She dodged trees and flew over streams, then careened up the mountainside to the land Erik had bought when they had first arrived in America.

From what he had told her, Mya was expecting untamed forest. Yet, as she crested the mountain, she found a large area of cleared land where a cabin-style house overlooked a lake. She gasped, and her body slowed to a stop as she approached the door. It reminded her so much of the cabin back in England that it was almost as if she had been transported back there. A million questions formed in her mind, but she shook them away. She would ask Erik about this later, once she knew he was safe.

She could smell his scent all over the property, but it engulfed her when she opened the door. The strength of it told her that he had been there recently, and her heartbeat raced at the thought of being able to see him, to hold him, to put the horrible events of today behind them.

Mya let his scent guide her as she ran through the house, until she ended in a room at the back of the property. It was sparsely furnished with a bed, chair, dresser, mirror, and desk which had a candle that was still burning.

She stepped closer to the desk and her heart plummeted. There, in the center of the desk, was Erik's ring, and underneath a letter addressed to her.

Shakily, she picked up the ring, which was still warm to the touch and opened the letter.

"My dearest fagr skjaldmær min,

I've known for a long time that you were unhappy. You've made the best of our time over the years. You always promised to wait, and I was foolish enough to take advantage of your patience. I am so sorry. I am sorrier than you will ever know. I never wanted to take advantage of you. I only wished to keep you safe, to love you, to cherish you, to marry you and now—

I saw you with him, and even though my heart aches, I cannot blame you. I only wish I'd done better. If I could turn back the hands of time, I would, I swear to you I would. But now what's done is done, and if someone else has your heart then I cannot jeopardize that, for your heart is one of the purest, most beautiful things I have ever known.

I love you, Mya. I will always love you. But if I stay around you, I will take you. I will ruin this for my own selfish needs, and I can't do that. I shouldn't be selfish with you, not anymore.

I wanted so much with you, fagr skjaldmær min. I used to wear this ring to ward off women. When they would ask me about my wife, I would tell them how beautiful she was, how special and radiant. In my heart, in my eyes, you will always be my wife, my mate, the place I run home to, but I understand that I can no longer be those things for you.

I may have squandered my chances, but I hope he gives you what you deserve--marriage, a home, a family--everything you've always wanted. And until then, know that this property is yours. I was building it for us, but even if there is no future for me here, there should be for you. You will find the keys, deed, and all necessary paperwork signed and sealed in the drawer. I have transferred all my assets to you in the hopes that you will live a life without struggle or strife.

This is goodbye, for there is no life without you, fagr skjaldmær min, my beautiful shield maiden, my beautiful warrior. You are one of the fiercest, bravest, most beautiful, most radiant women I have ever known.

With my entire heart and soul; yours forever,
Erik."

Mya clutched the letter and ring to her chest, standing in absolute silence while her heart shattered into a million pieces.

She didn't know how long she stayed like that—frozen into place, barely breathing—but when she came to and saw that the candle was sputtering, she knew there was only one thing she could do. She had to find him and tell him that none of it had been real. They were supposed to be together, live out their lives together. She was going to marry him, bear his children, spend the rest of her life by his side. That had always been their future. She knew it in her soul, which meant this horrible reality that left her heart barren and her entire being ripped to shreds simply could not exist.

No. She would find him. She would show him that what he saw was nothing but a trick, and then they would get retribution, together. They would marry, and the whole heartbreaking ordeal would become nothing more than a bitter memory. That was the only possibility she believed in.

Determined, she made her way through the house, searching for any sign of him. Finding nothing, she moved outside. Following his scent, she called his name while she searched through the forest. When she reached the cliffs, her mouth dropped open at the scene in front of her.

All the trees and brush were gone. In their place were mounds of ash, mixing with the scent of her beloved, her husband. There was nowhere else to go, no other trail to follow and nothing else to search for. His scent stopped by the cliff's edge. The pieces all fit together to create one unbelievable horror in her mind: Erik was gone. Dead. He'd thrown himself over the cliff, committed suicide, all because he'd thought he lost her, because of cruel revenge against someone who had done nothing to deserve it, because she hadn't gotten there in time to stop him, to make him see reason.

If she had just been faster, stronger, listened to the worry that had been weighing her down since that morning, he'd be here now. But she hadn't and now, now he was—

Mya screamed. She screamed louder than the waves that crashed along the cliff, louder than the force of the wind. She screamed so loud that the birds scattered, and she kept screaming as she crashed to her knees in the ash, clutching his letter and ring. She knew nothing else but agony, desperation, and despair. She wanted nothing else but to join him, to give everything up and simply fall away with him, hoping that maybe in another life, another world or dimension, they could have their happy ending. That was the only way to end this pain.

Mya stood slowly, then turned toward the cliff edge. She slipped Erik's ring on her thumb. It was too big, but she curled her fingers over it, pressing the metal into place. She'd keep it close even as she fell and met her death at the rocks deep below.

Then a waft of smoke filled Mya's nostrils, and she turned her head in its direction, searching for the cause.

Her first thought was that it had to be Erik, that he was still alive and she had just overlooked something. She could still be with him, still show him that she loved him. She could still *save* him.

Mya sped toward the scent, but as she drew closer, she found the large house that she hadn't known existed until only a few minutes ago, the place that Erik said he'd built for her, for *them*, was now engulfed in flames, and for the third time that day Mya was powerless to stop the chaos and destruction around her.

This wasn't right. It wasn't *fair!* They hadn't done

anything to deserve this! Erik had worked so hard to create a council that would help end all the killings and atrocities of their world. It was supposed to represent everyone, to fix things, but for all his efforts, this is what he'd gotten—what they'd gotten—in return: Tragedy. Heartbreak. Pain.

No.

No more.

Mya would not let it continue. She was going to die. She knew that, she *accepted* it, but she would not go before she got revenge for Erik and before she killed the people who did this to them.

The smell of the fire was overwhelming now, but Erik had taught her how to use her senses, how to keep and control her blood lust. Closing her eyes and rubbing her index finger on the warm metal of Erik's ring, Mya called on her practiced control of ferocious violence.

It wanted blood, and so it sought it out. Mya had scared the animals in the forest with her cries of anguish, so when she searched for the nearest source with the greatest amount of blood, she found exactly who she was looking for—the person who had set fire to their home.

The witch was laughing manically as she twirled around, droplets of blood flying from her dress. From her spot behind a large oak, Mya saw a slaughtered moose, its blood taken by the woman who now seemed to be celebrating what she'd done.

"One more vampire taken care of! One more gone!"

she sang, laughing and jumping and throwing her hands to the sky.

Mya wanted to snap her neck—she even reached out to do so—until she remembered that this blood witch wasn't the only one to blame for what had happened. No, their entire coven was. If Mya wanted to find them and exact her retribution, she would have to wait for this one to lead her to their home. There, she would kill them, every single last one, and only then would she be at peace.

CHAPTER 12

Mya followed the blood-drunk witch for two days.

The woman believed she was unstoppable. She used her powers recklessly, performing magic in front of humans only to wipe their minds of it afterward. As Mya watched, she realized just how powerful the witch was, and yet her powers never affected Mya.

Satisfaction pooled in Mya's gut with the knowledge that she was immune to the blood witch's power. If this witch couldn't affect her, it was likely that none of her coven's powers would be able to either. Mya wanted them to be powerless. She wanted them to know that a big, bad monster was coming for them, and nothing they could do would save them. She wanted them to feel the same way she felt, to know the same pain she had known when she lost the only man she had ever and would ever love. Every day, every second that went by was another in which she fed that pain to her anger, her rage, and her soon unavoidable wrath.

Finally, the witch went home, leading Mya to her coven. The house was set back in the poorest section of the city, an old, seemingly abandoned Gothic church. A fitting place for them to die, Mya thought, because there wasn't a single god who could save their worthless souls. Not from her.

Mya knocked on the large wooden door and waited. When it opened, she came face to face with the woman who'd been with Erik's impostor. The witch's eyes grew wide as fear morphed her expression into one of horror, and the reaction made Mya smile. The woman opened her mouth to scream, but before she could make a sound Mya reached forward, grabbed her by her neck and crushed her throat. The woman's eyes bulged before she fell to the ground, dead.

Mya stepped over her body, entering the foyer. Her eyes darted around the room, preparing for an attack, but instead she found four more witches, their mouths also agape in horror. It only made her smile wider.

"You have the gall to look at me as if you don't know why I'm here." Mya's eyes narrowed, and her tone turned bitter. "You took everything from me, and now, I am going to return the favor."

Mya killed them before they could blink, and she killed the next two who entered the room. One of them tried some sort of magic on her, and for that Mya broke her fingers, then her hand, her wrist, and her arm. Mya made the woman scream for even attempting to raise a hand to her, all before she tore her head from her neck and threw it onto the dusty floor.

The commotion brought forth more witches, and Mya killed them savagely. Each drop of their blood fueled her rage, her wrath, her need for vengeance and justice. No matter how many she killed, she could never bring Erik back, so she killed them in his name, in *their* name.

Room by room she slaughtered them. Some, after hearing the screams of their sisters, took up weapons to defend themselves, and a dark, deep part of Mya gained satisfaction after killing them with their own tools. At one time she had held *pity* for these creatures, for the atrocities committed against them, but now? Now they deserved every bit of the killer she'd become.

Mya reached the second to last closed door of the floor she was on. She kicked it open, ready to pounce, but the sight before her turned her blood cold. In the room were a dozen bassinets each containing a tiny, delicate newborn. The babies were mixed, not only human but different immortal species as well. Not a single child made a sound, and as Mya approached them, she felt the sparkle of magic, and knew they must be under some sort of spell.

She sensed a presence behind her and spun, then grabbed the young girl from the doorway and threw her back against the wall.

"Please! Wait!" she begged through broken breaths.

Mya's grip tightened on the girl's throat. "Whose children are these?"

"T-The wit-witches'."

Mya loosened her grip around the girl's neck slightly, then looked her over. She was young, with long blonde hair that was tangled and matted. She had bruises, dirt, and blemishes all over her skin, marring her otherwise cream complexion.

"Please," she begged. "I'm not like them. I'm not, I swear!"

Mya had been fooled before, and no matter how abused this girl might look, she did not want to be fooled again. "Tell me about the children," she ordered, hoisting the girl higher against the wall.

Her eyes bulged, but she made no move to defend herself or remove Mya's hand from around her throat. "They're children the blood witches had with immortals!"

"It's rare for immortals to have children. How are there so many?" she hissed.

The girl shook her head frantically. "These children aren't from normal births. The witches, they do something to immortals, then they sleep with them and kill them. Once they give birth, and the child reaches a certain age, they brand them and teach them blood magic."

The girl held her wrist in front of Mya's face. "Here, this is where they brand those that are taught blood magic. See? I don't have a brand. I'm not like them.

Please believe me," she cried.

Mya's eyes narrowed. "And who's to say you're not branded elsewhere and this isn't all a ploy?"

"I know who you are! I know what they did to you, Mya, and to Erik." Her panicked voice dropped to a whisper when Mya tightened her hand around the girl's neck again.

"Do not *ever* mention his name to me. You have no right!" Mya screamed.

The girl whimpered and her hand gripped Mya's begging her to loosen her hold. "I didn't kill him! But I know what they did, and I know why you're here. If you need to kill me or the others, I understand, but please leave the babies. They didn't do anything wrong."

Mya didn't loosen her hold, but she didn't tighten her grasp either. "Others? What others?"

"Th-There are other girls like me who take care of the babies. We were all shackled, but I was the last one to look over the children, so I was free. None of us are blood witches."

"And after you're done taking care of these children, then what? What do you get out of it?" Mya snarled.

The girl looked down, so Mya shook her, drawing her gaze back.

"Death," she croaked as tears clouded her eyes.

Mya's eyes widened. She let the girl go and watched as she dropped to the ground on her knees. "Explain."

The girl was shaking. Whether it was from fear or weakness, Mya didn't know, but after several gulps of air she finally spoke. "They don't change us into blood witches. They abduct us, normally from traveling colonies, and then they make us take care of their children. Once we've served our purpose, they kill us."

The girl shook her head and looked up at Mya, her big green eyes now filled with determination. "It doesn't matter if you kill me. I'm dead already, but those children didn't do anything."

Mya reached down to the girl, but she shied away, cowering against the wall.

"Please, I-I can give you more. They were going to after your brother, Greg, and Luke. Please believe me!"

Mya drew in a sharp breath. Her heart beat frantically at the thought of losing her brother and cousin. The pounding was so strong it felt as if it would come out of her chest. Her whole world flipped, faded, and crashed on its side.

Get it together! Now isn't the time to fall apart.

Mya grabbed the girl by the chin. The sudden move made her gasp, and Mya leaned over her. "What is your name?"

"E-Elaine."

"Elaine, if you're lying to me about any of this, I will take my time with you. I will break every bone in your body, heal you, and do it all over again. Do you understand?"

Elaine gulped and nodded.

Mya straightened and dropped her hand from her. "Are there any more blood witches?"

"N-No, not here. But there are wards in the cemetery. If any of the witches escaped, they'd go there."

"And do you have what you need here to free the other girls and prepare the children for travel?"

"Y-Yes."

"Then go. Make sure to change your clothes and have the others do the same, then meet me in front of the church."

Elaine blinked for a moment, then stood. Slowly she moved around Mya, constantly checking behind her as if to make sure Mya wouldn't change her mind and kill her, until she finally scurried from the room.

With one last look at the babies, Mya made her way back through the house, over the bodies of the witches she'd killed, and out to the cemetery. There she found five more witches, but she killed them with less vigor than before. Now it wasn't just about Erik; it was about protecting her family. She was more cautious, more precise, and for her efforts she found an additional four witches she would have otherwise missed in her violent haze. Mya picked up their bodies and hauled them into the church.

She had just finished with the women when Elaine met her, as instructed, along with six other young girls. Most held two babies in their arms. The girls themselves looked terrible, covered bruises and cuts like Elaine, but at least they were dressed, and that would be enough for Mya get them to the tavern without too many questions.

Mya gestured for the girls to move back, and then she lit the house on fire. She stood and watched it burn. The fire brought back the picture of Erik's house—their house—and it was as if the flames burned away at Mya's retribution. Suddenly she felt tired, like the weight of the world had finally engulfed her, and the pain she felt went deeper than her skin, her mind, and her heart. It was etched into her very soul.

Someone tapped on her shoulder and Mya spun around, making Elaine gasp.

"I-I just wanted to give this to you. I didn't know your size, but I thought it might help if you changed too."

Mya took the blood red material, trying to keep her hand from shaking. She wiped the blood from her face, hair, and chest, then she pulled off her dress and threw it in the fire. After she'd shucked on the gown Elaine had given her, she gave the girl a curt nod in thanks.

The group walked together until Mya could flag several carriages, paying handsomely for their discretion. Once in the carriage, she grasped her shaking hands tightly, gulping in air and tasting the foul smells of horse shit, blood, filth, and alcohol. They were her reminders that she was here, still alive. She had to be, just for a little bit longer.

They arrived at the tavern, and Greg pulled the door open before Mya could raise her hand. His brows were twisted, his eyes glowing red, and her breath hitched.

"Where have you been? I've been looking all over for

you! You were supposed to come right back! Do you have any idea—"

The dam inside her broke open and the tide dragged her under. "Greg," she hiccupped. "He's dead. Erik's dead!" Then the whole world tilted, and she welcomed the endless black.

CHAPTER 13

"Your sister killed an entire coven of witches!" Francois, one of the council members, shouted.

"And if she hadn't, we would all be dead!" Greg yelled.

The council meeting had been going on for hours. After Mya collapsed in Greg's arms, he carried her upstairs. Then he took care of Elaine and the rest of the girls. Along with Luke, he set up a nursery for the babies, and when Mya awoke, he held her while she told him everything that had happened.

Mya stayed in that room, staring vacantly at the wall, sitting on the bed she had shared with Erik only a few short days prior. She didn't move, didn't eat, didn't drink, or sleep until Greg told her they had to report what happened to the newly formed council. Mya followed him wordlessly. Now that she had no one to hunt or kill, nothing to investigate and no reason or purpose or fuel for revenge, the fight had left her body. and all she felt was numb.

The fighting started the moment Greg had told The Council what she had done. Arguments broke out about how unstable she was, how she couldn't be trusted, how she deserved to be punished, and perhaps they were right. After all, she did destroy an entire coven, and she would do it again without a second thought. In fact, she held no remorse for what she'd done. She only wished she'd destroyed them before they had destroyed her, before they had broken her heart and ripped out the very essence of her soul: her beloved, Erik.

"You know our laws," Francois snarled.

"I know them because *I* made them," Greg barked back.

Mya looked at Greg, studying him. For most of the meeting he'd been calm, patient, explanatory, but in the last few minutes he'd become more and more upset, and now he sounded as if he wanted to pounce on the man and tear him limb from limb.

"Then you also know that we cannot make an exception just because this woman is your own flesh and blood."

Greg hissed. "Francois—"

"Do not make an exception for me," Mya said blankly, tired of the arguing, tired of being in this world when Erik was not. "If you must punish me, do so."

Francois's eyes turned to hers, and for a moment she swore she saw delight in them. "Then you admit you should die for what you've done."

Mya's eyes widened in shock, not horror. Francois was offering her exactly what she wanted. Her death would set her free, allow her to pass on from the cruel fate of living here without Erik.

"Mya—" Greg started, only to be interrupted by Francois.

"She savagely destroyed an entire coven of witches. This council was created by you and Erik as a haven for all immortals. If we leave her alive, the message it sends to others is that vampires are still superior and this council will protect them above all others." His eyes narrowed. "We cannot trust that she will not do this again. I vote death as Mya's punishment."

Lily snapped her fan closed. "Francois, you are forgetting why these deaths occurred. The witches killed first—"

"We have no guarantee that Erik is dead. We have not begun an investigation to ensure that he is, which is required *before* any vote for punishment," Greg bit out.

Mya wanted to argue. She opened her mouth to do so, to accept the sweet gift of death, but Francois spoke first.

"And what then? What guarantee do we have that you wouldn't hide your sister to save her?"

Greg took a step forward. "I would never—"

"You have a conflict of interest—"

Lily smacked the table with her fan. "Enough!" she ordered, and everyone fell silent. "Francois is correct. This was genocide, and it is not what we stand for, not anymore."

Greg started. "Mya—"

Lily shot him a look that stalled the rest of his words. "Losing Erik has created a large void for all of us, but no one feels that void stronger than Mya. She is —*was*—his mate."

Mya's head snapped up at the word and she met Lily's gaze. "His mate?"

Lily's eyes widened. "He never told you?" she asked, sighing and pinching her brow as Mya shook her head. "By the gods," she whispered under her breath. "Mya, immortals have mates, partners who they are the most compatible with. It's different for everyone. Some are fated, destined to be together, while others can be rejected. But it is clear from what you felt, from what you've *done*, that Erik was your fated mate."

This knowledge tugged at something in her, something dark and broken. This was just another thing she didn't know, another thing she should have known, another *secret*. "W-What does that mean?" she asked.

"It means that Erik is the only person you would have ever loved or truly been happy with. He's also the only person you could procreate with."

Erik's ring felt warm on her finger, the opposite of the coldness that swept through her body. Mya looked around the room dumbfounded, taking in the faces of sadness, anger, righteousness and pity. Then her gaze landed on Greg and Elaine. "But the blood witches—"

"They tampered with the immortal's fated line," Lily said.

"Which is dangerous," a council member snarled.

"Mya saved us by killing those witches. We could have lost the ability to find our fated mates," another member followed.

"And how will we be able to explain that to the witch council when one of us can extinguish their entire line? When a council member's *sister* has already done so? Do you really believe they wouldn't try to use this as an excuse for war?" Francois said.

Several members of The Council grunted and nodded in agreement.

"I've heard and understand your grievances," Greg said sternly, causing Mya to shift her gaze to his. "I ask that you allow me to investigate Erik's death, as written in our laws."

"There is nothing to investigate! Erik's reaction to believing his fated mate rejected him is understandable, but there has never been a record in all our history of a fated mate committing a massacre because of rejection. Those actions have only ever been committed when the mate has passed. And she said it herself, she tracked him over a cliff!" Francois exclaimed, his pale, powdered skin growing as red as a tomato.

"Regardless," Greg said through clenched teeth, "if

we must uphold the law for death then we must uphold the law for investigation."

"And you plan to lead it yourself so you can use your position to hide information and run circles around the rest of us? No, I don't think so," Francois said.

"You're absolutely correct," Greg said, drawing a gasp from everyone, including Mya. "It is not fair that I should run the investigation while being a council member. Until this is adjourned, I will remove myself from the position."

"Greg—" Mya began, but he held up his hand.

"Does that satisfy The Council?" he asked.

"And what guarantee do we have that this will be your top priority?" Francois asked.

"I will provide you with a report once a month."

"Once a week," Francois ordered.

"Fine," Greg said, his body vibrating with tightly controlled fury.

"You will also explain your sister's actions to the witch council. Should she ever do something so horrendous again, you will take her punishment."

Mya called out her brother's name, but Greg threw her a sharp glare before turning back to Francois. "Agreed."

The moment they walked out of the meeting hall, Mya grabbed Greg's arm. "Why did you do that for me?"

"I don't believe Erik's dead," Greg said, ripping his arm from her grasp and marching down the street on furious steps.

His words shocked her, and for a moment she stood still staring at his back, then raced after him.

"He is dead," she whispered at first, but then the raw emotion overwhelmed her and she screamed, "He's gone! Why would you want to investigate his death? Don't you get it? He left. He left me!"

Greg's eyes narrowed, hardened. "And what would you like me to do? Let you die over a possibility?"

"Yes! I would rather be dead. At least then I could be with him!"

His eyes flashed red, and darkness flew at them at such high speed that the wind chilled her. "I will never let that happen," he hissed.

"I wish you would!" Tears clouded her vision and rolled down her cheeks. She looked down at her trembling hands, saw Erik's metal ring, and her heart broke and bled until it was as dead as Erik. "There's nothing for me here. Nothing," she whispered.

Greg didn't say another word.

———

Days and months and years went by, and Mya did nothing.

She spent most of her time in a catatonic state where she simply stared outside and watched as the sun rose and set. She watched as time went by, as people laughed, ate, grew, fell in love, and died. She watched it all because Erik couldn't, and she knew he'd never see another day beside her.

Greg reminded her to eat. Luke did too, but it was Greg who would force blood down her throat when she got a little too close to the edge of starvation, and it was Greg who took the brunt of her anger every time he made her eat. He also took her anger, her rage and sorrow, every time he stopped her from killing herself.

She tried, by the gods how she'd tried. Her accursed power made it so most things that would at least weaken other vampires did nothing to her. She could go months without blood, direct wounds healed in an instant, and her body rejected poison. Mya tried to hang herself, but the rope broke most of the time, and on the few blessed occasions where it didn't Greg always found her and cut her down. She tried to drown herself; he saved her. She tried to shoot herself; when he realized she owned a gun he removed all the bullets without telling her, and then he removed anything she could use as a weapon until she had no choice but to sit in her misery and endure it.

One day, she watched from her window as someone threw out a hoe. Mya's sunken eyes widened at the chance. She raced downstairs and moved to open the door, only to find her brother. He had the same look on his face as always, a grim glare with a frown at his mouth, as if his disappointment in her was etched onto his skin. Without a word he picked her up and tossed her over his shoulder.

"Let me go!" she screamed, but he remained silent as he carried her upstairs. She pounded on his back, shouted and cried and cursed at him, and yet he still didn't say a word.

He sat her down firmly in her chair before turning to leave.

She yelled so loudly, lost and manic, "Why won't you let me die? Why won't you let me have peace? Why are you being so selfish—"

He laughed, a bitter chuckle that seemed to come from deep inside him, then he turned around to face her with so much fire in her eyes that she drew back for a moment.

"Selfish? I'm selfish? I'm not the one fucking dreaming of killing themselves to try and reunite with a man who might not even be dead!"

Mya rose from her seat. "Don't. Don't you dare say that! He's gone, and the fact that you can't accept that—"

"If that isn't rich coming from you. I can accept that he's gone. I accept it every day that I wake up and breathe this air and have to come to this house to see if today is the day I will find my sister's lifeless body," Greg growled.

Mya threw her arms out as she screamed, "I didn't ask you to take care of me!"

Greg's eyes narrowed. "You're right. You didn't ask me to take care of you, but that's what family does. You may have forgotten we exist in all your grief and pain.

You may believe there's nothing left for you here. None of us may matter to you, but I'm not going to give up on you. Hate me all you want, but that will never happen, Mya."

Her eyes stung and his form became blurry under the trail of hot tears as the monster of chaos within her surged to the height of a rogue tidal wave. "Greg—"

He shook his head. With an exasperated sigh, he turned to leave.

"I don't hate you!" she choked, reaching out to him even though she stood stuck, unable to make herself embrace him.

Greg froze.

"I don't hate you," she whispered, "but I have nothing here."

"You have a family, Mya!" Greg shouted so loudly that she swore the whole house shook. "You have a brother and a cousin that love and adore you and want to help protect and save you with every fiber of their beings, but you won't let us! For years all you cared about was Erik!"

"You wouldn't understand!"

"Then make me. Since I don't understand, make me."

The house shook again as Greg's power drew in the energy and shadows around her. The weight of it was so heavy she could barely breathe, barely stand.

"He was my everything, my whole heart, and without him here it feels like it's gone. It feels like my entire heart is vacant, and I can't get that back, Greg. I *can't.*"

Her nails dug into her chest as she tore at where her heart should have been, just as her brother had torn the explanation from her, like each word was cutting through her flesh and bone.

"No, you won't *try* to get it back. There's a difference, Mya. He was your everything and you were his, and the way he was taken from you was a horrific tragedy, but you weren't the only one that lost him! My grief can never compare to yours, and neither can Luke's, but we can understand a fraction of it. Yet, you won't let us. You won't move past your pain. Once upon a time your family meant everything to you, and now we mean *nothing.*"

"Greg, please, no. Don't say that!" Mya cried, but for all her words she still couldn't move to embrace him, to reach out to him and comfort him.

"But it's the truth," he said, and his eyes clouded over with grief. "The moment you lost Erik, we lost you, and we're not enough to pull you back. You won't even let us try!"

She shook her head frantically. That wasn't the truth. How could it be, when watching and listening to his pain hurt her so? And yet, she hadn't shown him anything different. She didn't even know how to, and it sickened her to face the fact that he was correct. She didn't want to try. She wanted the world to forget about her, to let her live in her burdens and misery in peace until she died.

"Greg, just leave me here. Let me live in my pain," she said with a sad smile. "That's all I'm good for—"

"No!" He stormed toward her and bared down on her with such ferocity that she felt as though the world stopped moving. "No. You don't get to say that. I will *not* listen to you sit here and say that. You have a gift, Mya. There is so much you could do, and yet you sit in your fucking chair and squander your life away out of grief. You are worth the sun and the moon. You are my sister, but the woman you've turned into is not the woman I know. Where is the girl who was brave, who would fight, who faced every single adversity? Where did she go?"

Tears rolled down her cheeks as she whispered, "She grew tired. She died."

"No, she gave up. That's what you did, Mya, you gave up."

She snapped. "You act like this is so easy, like I can just flip a switch and become something else. He *died*, Gregori. He died!" she screeched so loudly that spit landed on his face.

Mya pushed him, punched and kicked at him, but he grabbed her and brought her close. She chanted her last words into his chest as her heart broke even further, as she turned raw, drowning in grief and rage and hatred and sorrow. Greg simply rubbed her back, her hair, and comforted her even as she attacked him.

Eventually she grew quiet.

"Do you want a reason to live, to become that woman again? Do you want to have a purpose?" he said into her hair.

"What could I do? What could I be used for?" she murmured into his chest.

"I'll show you."

Over the centuries Greg built his circle—carefully under The Council's watchful eye—and Mya helped him do it.

She helped him turn and trained the new recruits, people who could be trusted like Elaine, Merida, and Dominick. She fought in their battles, their wars, she chased down rogue vampires and killed them. With each person's life she took, she saved another potential mate, another innocent, another person who wouldn't have to face what she had.

Mya learned efficient business practices, coding, how to create official documentation for their companies, how to track, navigate, how to hunt whatever, *whoever,* was her prey that week. She was ruthless because she could afford to be. She fought without conscious, like she had already died, because she had.

A purpose didn't save her. It didn't renew her or bring her back to life, but it gave her something to channel her emotions, her power, and her specific abilities into. But on the days when everything was quiet, when she couldn't sleep, when she watched someone else fall into the deep love she'd once had, she grew cold and fell into her dark misery all over again.

On those days, she hated her purpose.

On those days, she hated her brother even more.

CHAPTER 14

It had been 110,308 days since the last time Mya saw Erik.

She'd mourned him for every single one of those days, until eight months ago when she found out he was still alive. According to Johanna, he *had* to still be alive because an evil bitch named Constance had used him as her own personal guinea pig.

In those eight months, Mya had wrecked the city. She'd turned over every block, every stone, but she still hadn't found him. The only things she had to keep her hopes up were her family and Johanna's word that Constance and her band of minions needed Erik.

Logically, Mya knew that if anyone had gotten their hands on an elder vampire who was now over one thousand years old, they would, of course, keep them alive, if for nothing else than simply the history in their mind and the blood in their veins.

But this was Erik. *Her* Erik. The same man that she had shrines and portraits of in her home so that she didn't forget his face. The same man that she kept memories of in journals, re-writing them as the pages faded. She remembered key moments: the day he saved her life, the first day she felt something different toward him, the first time he'd kissed her, trained her, confessed his love for her. She remembered the day she lost him. Mya would never forget that pain and agony. She'd thought she would never see him again, and now she knew there was a chance she might.

Mya had never been good at having hope or faith, but she would pray to every old and new god if it meant she could see Erik just one more time, if she could hold him in her arms. But eight months of searching had yet to yield anything.

She knew Erik had been alive when they had faced off against Zachariah, and that he had been held in the same area as Johanna before Zachariah had dragged her out. But that cave had been buried under the explosives Zachariah had set, and the mountain was too unstable to explore.

Daniella wanted to use her magic to investigate the area, but it was too risky, especially while she was pregnant. Even though Mya wanted to find Erik, she didn't want it to be at the expense of her friend, unborn niece, and, by extension, her brother. So, she waited, searched, located, and interrogated every rogue vampire she could find, but they were too crazed to give her any answers.

Johanna tried to help as well, but it mostly resulted in rogue vampires coming after her to try and drag her back to Constance. She'd offered to use herself as bait, but everyone, including Mya, had shut the idea down. Even though Mya had mostly ignored Johanna when they first found her—because of how much she reminded her of Erik—she was Luke's mate and she'd become a close friend. Johanna had gone through far too much, and Mya was not willing to subject her to any more.

Johanna enlisted her younger sister, Tamara, who was hiding out in the Fae Realm with her family under Loe's protection, to see if they could help. But even there, with all the powers and resources of the Fae Realm, they couldn't find anything.

It wasn't until Daniella gave birth to Mya's niece, Ruby Adalyn Novak, a beautiful girl with her mother's brown skin tone and her father's hazel eyes, that things changed. Daniella refused to rest, and within days she began investigating the caves.

While Daniella grew tired easily, Johanna's mental ability helped her fortify her strength. Over time they were able to search further and further, until they eventually located the cage Erik had been held in. Based on what Daniella could tell from the vines she used to feel around the bars, it had been broken open from the inside out. When Daniella didn't find any bodies near that entrance, Mya breathed a sigh of relief. Erik had at least made it out on his own, but that didn't answer the question of where he was now.

Daniella pulled several items out of the cave, including a partial map that Mya was now combing over. It was nothing more than lines and dashes, with a few small hand drawn markers. Mya had tried to plot out the distances, but they didn't make sense, and none of the lines, which she figured must be some sort of route system, corresponded to any type of geographical location. She also discovered another partial map in some paperwork Luke had found when he was searching for Johanna. The maps seemed to match, but it was clear there was still a large portion missing. and she hadn't been able to figure it out on her own, nor with the help of any of the databases she had hacked into. There was something there, she knew there was, but she couldn't see it, and it felt as if her heart was breaking all over again with each day that went by without finding Erik.

Mya sighed, her whole body curling into itself over the map. She massaged her temples and closed her eyes. The deep breaths she took should have helped, but they only felt like a waste of time. Mya remembered all the times Greg had tried to beat into her head that she could cause as much chaos as she wanted, but if she couldn't calm the storm when she needed to be mindful and take care of herself, she wouldn't live long enough to find Erik in the first place.

"That bad, huh?"

Mya looked up to see Greg leaning against the door-frame with his daughter in his arms. For a second she wondered if she had manifested him with her thoughts.

No. He probably just has a homing beacon for when I need a dose of reality to kick my ass back into gear.

"Yeah," she confessed.

"When was the last time you took a break?" he asked, walking into the room while gently patting Ruby's back.

"It's been..." She checked her watch and gulped as she realized that over four hours had passed since she'd last moved.

"Thought so. Here, let's trade."

He carefully laid Ruby into Mya's arms and took the maps from her, settling down in the chair across from her. Mya smiled down at her niece's beautiful, scrunched face. She loved her so deeply, so fiercely. It was a type of love she didn't know she could ever feel again, but Ruby also reminded her of all the things she wanted, all the things she once thought she'd have by now.

Ruby cooed, wiggling and kicking her little feet. Realizing she was beginning to fuss, Mya started to softly hum the melody of a song that she'd written one night when she couldn't sleep. It was a heartbreaking song about love and loss, about watching the figure she dreamed of disappearing the moment she opened her eyes.

When Ruby fell asleep, Mya looked to Greg and found him staring back at her.

"I haven't heard you do that in a while."

"What?"

"Hum. Sing. I didn't even know you still did." His hazel eyes looked back at the map as a frown creased his forehead.

Mya fidgeted slightly in the chair, embarrassed. "I do it sometimes when I can't sleep."

"And how often is that?"

"Most nights." She shrugged gently, but she could feel the weight of her brother's stare, the careful assessment of her that he took, as if he could see into her mind, her soul.

Greg flicked a piece of the map, studying it. "I thought that had gotten better."

"It's never really gone away. Some days it's better, some days it's not."

He let out a soft *hmm*, eyes still on the map.

"Greg?" she said, calling his attention. When his eyes met hers, she swallowed down the ball in her throat. She knew it would be hard to say her next words, but she had to. He deserved them. "You were right. You were right about Erik being alive, and you were right when you said I had given up all those years ago."

He looked at her, as if he could tell how much she struggled to start the conversation, but still he said nothing.

"How did you know? About him, I mean. Why did you believe he was still alive?"

He clasped his hands and settled further in the chair. "Because he loved you, Mya. When Erik asked me for my blessing, it was to look after you, take care of you, to keep you as his number one priority. It was never to be *with* you. In all the years we were together, he never took your love for granted. He never expected you to love him, to *choose* him, and he was willing to force himself to be content with just being by your side if that was what you wanted. Your happiness and safety came first to him, which is the same reason I was willing to give him my blessing."

Tears gathered in Mya's eyes, but she refused to let them fall.

Greg leaned forward and squeezed her arm. "Now that I'm older and I have more experience, I understand mate bonds. I can only try to understand what Erik felt when he thought you rejected him. I believe he wrote the goodbye letter to you because his want, his desperate need to protect you was prevalent in his words, but leaving you? Committing suicide? No."

"Erik was my mentor and my closest friend, but he would never have trusted me to look after you. Even with a broken heart he would have stayed by your side. He would have never left you alone, even if that meant staying in the shadows where you couldn't find him. I'm just sorry that the both of you had to go through this much and end up here."

Mya tried to cover her mouth as sobs began to rack her. She felt her brother take the weight of Ruby from her. She heard him step outside the room, and then he was back, holding her close to his chest.

"I'm sorry," she murmured into his shoulder. "I'm so sorry for all the times that I—"

"I know," he said, his voice laced with pain. "I know there have been times you've hated me, and I know our relationship has never been as good as it once was, but that doesn't make me love you any less, Mya. You'll always be my sister, and I'm sorry for all the times I was hard on you. I know that didn't help."

She wiped at her eyes and shook her head. "No, I deserved that. I needed that. If you had coddled me, I would've stayed in my sorrowful little state and never tried to do anything with my life. Because of you I now have a chance. You fighting with me gave me that."

He smiled, and his warmth broke through some of the darkness surrounding her heart. "If you need someone to fight with or for you, I'm always happy to do so. I love you, Mya, and I will always do anything I can to help you, no matter how difficult you might make it."

"Thank you for always being there, and I love you too."

A soft knock on the open door broke Mya and Greg apart, and Mya smiled as Daniella walked in and dropped a kiss on Mya's head, then turned to kiss Greg.

"Hey sweetheart," he said as he wrapped his arm around her waist.

"Good morning, love." Daniella smiled at Greg, and there was so much adoration in her eyes that it felt as if Mya were intruding on a special moment between them. It was equally heartwarming and heart-wrenching for Mya to watch. If Gregori was a king, Daniella was his queen. If he was the patriarch, the father of their circle, Daniella was the matriarch, the elemental mother—equally kind, protective, and wrathful to anyone who hurt their family.

She simply fit in a way that was astonishing to witness, and that extended to her place in the entire circle. Daniella had the respect, admiration, and devotion of every single one of their battle officers, warriors who could be difficult to please. She'd become someone they went to for advice, someone who aided them whenever possible, and an incredible fighter that Mya was proud to battle alongside. But even more than that, Daniella had changed Greg.

Mya had seen the same thing with Johanna. Luke was calmer, more positive, serene in a way Mya had never seen before. There were immortals with mates, but the changes she'd watched her family and their other halves go through over the last year were incredible to witness, and Mya had to admit to a small bit of jealousy, of longing. Had she been that way when Erik was around? Was that why his loss was so potent, why it had changed her so? And what would happen when she found him?

What would happen if she didn't?

Mya looked at the maps again with renewed vigor. She had to find him, and once she did, she'd get him to Johanna to restore his memories. She just had to—

"Let me see those," Daniella said, and Mya stood and pulled back her chair to let her sit down.

"There's something there. I can feel it. It's like there's magic I can't see in between the pages," Greg said.

Mya's eyes widened and she moved to look over Daniella's shoulder. She gasped as she realized that she'd been so focused on finding Erik, on making the maps mean something she could understand, that she'd missed the aura surrounding them. It was only a tingle, like static electricity, but it was there.

Daniella fingered the corner of one of the maps. "You won't be able to see it because it isn't meant for you," she said breathlessly.

"The spirits?" Greg asked, rubbing Daniella's back.

She nodded. "We need Johanna and Luke."

***

"What did you find?" Johanna asked when she and Luke approached the table, breathless and still charged of energy from teleporting to them.

"Tell me what you feel," Daniella said, tapping the map.

Johanna ran her fingers over the edges, then gasped, pulling them back. "It's filled with magic. Witch magic."

Mya looked from Greg to Luke, only to find that they seemed to be just as confused as she was. "What are you two talking about?"

"This map is imbued with witch magic, but in a way that no spell or immortal can access." Daniella's eyes touched Mya's then Greg's. "No matter how long either of you spent reviewing it, you would never have been able to see the true contents of the map."

Mya gasped.

Luke stepped forward. "Wait a second, I've never heard of anyone being able to do that."

"It's extremely high-level magic," Greg said, crossing his arms. "Could it be familial?"

Johanna shook her head. "No, a witch's magic is similar to an immortal's. It needs purposeful intention and energy. The fact that this is still emitting magic either means that Constance has touched it recently, which we know couldn't possibly be true, or that it's spelled."

Daniella nodded. "And I believe the way to break the spell is with blood. Your blood, Johanna."

Johanna tilted her head to the side. "My blood?"

"Or Luke's. Both of you have been infected with Constance's blood, and I think this map only reveals its contents to someone who has received her blood."

Johanna and Luke looked at one another. His grip

on her waist tightened, and then Johanna asked, "Where do you need it?"

Mya watched as Daniella ran her fingers over the map. Nothing stood out to Mya, nor seemed different from one place to another, but Daniella eventually paused and said, "Here."

Mya edged closer as Johanna pricked her index finger with one of her fangs. She hovered her finger over the spot, then let several drops of blood fall where Daniella had indicated.

At first, nothing seemed to happen, then the aura around the map grew stronger. The air seemed to vibrate as the map began to illuminate. Before Mya's eyes, mountains, forests, and buildings began to appear. Their images grew stronger until the map was colored in rich and vibrant details. When the last of the images had settled, a thick black 'X' appeared, circled over one of the buildings. They all bent closer, scanning the map as best as they could.

Five seconds later, it burned to a crisp. But that didn't matter. For the first time in eight months, they had a lead.

***

The whole thing was a bust.

Mya and her family drove to the spot on the map, where they found a nightclub packed with people. Greg and Luke reluctantly stayed in their cars while Mya, Daniella, and Johanna went inside.

Johanna did a mental scan of the club members and

found who they were looking for immediately, but the men recognized them too. Six vampires stood and began to approach them. Mya, Johanna, and Daniella lured them outside to a back alley, and when the nightclub door shut, they killed everyone, save for the leader.

The man refused to speak. Johanna broke into his mind, planning to use her abilities to break the truth out of him, but there was nothing. It was as if his entire mind had been wiped clean. The moment she pulled out, the man's eyes widened and his head exploded, sending bits of matter everywhere. Then the dead vampires' heads did the same, leaving them staring at one another in shock.

Their group searched the immediate area to see if someone nearby had caused the explosions, but they found no one. At a loss, they went home, each with their mate—the other half of their soul—while Mya went home to an empty house.

She didn't blame her family. They had done their best. They tried to help, and they were just as disappointed as she was, but disappointment wasn't all she felt. She was in agony, enraged, and fed up with the entire world. Their lead, their first real lead, had taken them nowhere. They had absolutely nothing. *She* had absolutely nothing.

Mya couldn't sleep. She worked her way through the dark web, searching through forums. She ran background checks on the IDs of the immortals they'd killed, but she came up empty. Each ID was a fake, and the recognition software database she'd hacked into couldn't find anything on them either, not even a Missing Person's Report. It was as if they were ghosts.

Her hands shook, and she knew there was only one thing that could settle her for the night. She changed into black pants, a black tank top, leather jacket and boots. She filled her pockets with her usual weaponry—throwing knives, stars, dust, small containers of alcohol and gasoline, matches, a lighter, a collapsible staff—slipped Erik's ring and the necklace she kept it on into the hidden pocket within her jacket, picked up her sword and headed out to hunt.

***

Mya watched from the skyscraper, scanning the streets for rogue vampires. The wind howled around her and tugged strands of her hair from her braid as she waited. New York City was loud, even at night. The sounds of police sirens, ambulances, and the countless amount of people biking, walking, and talking never ceased. The city never slept, and because of that it was the perfect playground for immortals, whether they were sane or not.

A deep growl mixed with a mocking laugh echoed from her right—the sound of a predator trapping its prey—exactly what she was looking for.

She jumped from building to building, using her vampire speed to fly along the rooftops until she stood above the alleyway. She leaped down from the tall building, carefully timing her fall so that she landed directly onto the rogue vampire's head. Gravity took care of the rest, and his body folded in on itself—tendons snapping, bones breaking—until it resembled a pancake. It made her smile, and the poor human who would have been dead had it not been for Mya, exited the alleyway none the wiser.

Mya took down several other rogue vampires that way, both alone and in groups, but it still didn't ease the frantic beating of her heart. She was beginning to think nothing would, until she came across her third rogue vampire group and noticed that they were stabbing and cutting their victim. They normally preferred to tear their victims limb by limb while they drained them dry.

She sped forward, grabbed the nearest vampire, and pulled their arm back, breaking it in one motion. She moved so quickly that the others hadn't even sensed her presence until the vampire began to howl. He only got out a squeak of the sound before she stabbed him clean through his head.

The other vampires who turned toward her—teeth bared, faces contorted with murderous intent—died within the next two seconds. Then Mya got a look at the man they were trying to disembowel. He was an immortal. His hair was covered in dirt and blood, his face bruised, eyes sunken in, but for a single moment, they met hers, and time stopped.

It was Erik.

She'd found him.

CHAPTER 15

Mya did her best to carry Erik through the woods. More rogue vampires had appeared, so she'd been forced to deal with them first before attending to Erik. He'd fallen unconscious after the sixth man she killed. By the twentieth, his breath had become labored. It shouldn't have been possible. Erik was a vampire, an elder vampire at that, and one of the strongest men she'd ever known, but now he was dying on her back.

She wanted to check his wounds, to give him her blood, but she couldn't until she'd made sure they were safe. For that, she had to disguise their tracks. By the time she'd gotten him on her back, four more SUVs of rogue vampires had appeared. Mya could take them all, but each second she spent fighting them was another Erik spent bleeding out, and she would not risk him, *ever*.

She purposefully dragged her steps, letting the

weight of him fall into her to make sure the outlines of her shoes were more pronounced. Together they reached the river. Its current was strong, and while she didn't want the added risk, she knew they needed to cross it to help disguise their scent, so she waded through. She bent brush and discarded leaves, doing anything she could to throw them off the trail, but every moment they spent there was a delay. Erik was still unconscious, his blood coating her clothes, and she knew she had to finish this quickly. He didn't have much time left.

Mya found the entrance to a cave, breathing a small sigh of relief. It would serve as the perfect distraction for the vampires she was sure were tracking her, and where there was one cave entrance, there was always another. Hoisting Erik further up her back, Mya leaped onto the side of the mountain, then onto a tree. She traveled through the air until she spotted an opening that would work perfectly for them.

Slipping inside the cave, Mya traveled down the passageway until she reached a large stream of water. She hoped she'd gone deep enough. When she was sure that the cave was empty, she laid Erik down and truly looked at him.

He was nothing like the man she once knew.

His blonde hair had grown long, reaching down his back. Lengths of it were missing, as if it had been caught on something and torn. His face was ashen, his skin paler than she ever remembered it and covered in a layer of soot and blood. She ripped open his shirt to see his wounds and gasped at the deep cuts she found. Her fingers traveled over his chest, and she noted how malnourished he was. It was clear he'd been through hell, and as overjoyed as she was to finally have him in her arms, she was just as angry at his captors for what they'd done to him and at herself for not finding him sooner.

Erik didn't deserve this, but she would fix it. She'd fix it all.

Mya cut into her hand, letting the blade slide up her arm. She needed more blood than usual to cover as many of his wounds as possible at the same time. She held her healing magic back to stop it from sealing her own wound, then lined up her arm with three of the large gashes on his body and let the blood flow. Into it she pushed every ounce of her healing magic.

The wounds began to heal, but it was slower than usual. Too slow. Something must have been wrong with his blood, and because of how much he'd lost Mya couldn't heal both it and his wounds fast enough for him to survive.

There was only one other option; the one thing he had always told her not to do, because, as she now knew, it would trigger their mate bond.

She cut a line down her neck, bent over him, and lifted his lips to the spot. "Drink, please," she whispered. "Don't leave me now that I've found you."

———

"Don't leave me now that I've found you."

When was the last time Erik had heard words spoken to him with such anguish, with such worry and concern for him? The body pressed against his was warm. Her breasts were soft, like feathered pillows that he wanted to bury his head into, and the smell of her was divine, something of juniper, wildflowers, vanilla, and berries. He wanted to taste her, and that desire was so strong he began to salivate. He swallowed the drool, and then he tasted her blood in his mouth, her essence, and it felt as though the whole world had suddenly sharpened and turned vividly brilliant.

More of her blood slipped into his mouth, and he groaned at the taste.

"Drink, my love," she whispered, her voice like a caress that spread over his skin, chasing away the dark, the cold.

He couldn't deny her. Her throat vibrated against his lips, and he growled. His fangs lengthened and he bit down on her neck. His taste buds exploded as he drank from her, slurped more of her down. He couldn't tear himself away. Each gulp made him feel stronger, more powerful. He was captivated by her, enchanted, drunk on her essence and he needed more.

For the first time in centuries, he *desired* something. Someone. He wanted her etched into the very fabric of his being. He wanted her to coat the inside of his every cell, and he wanted to fuck her while she did it.

He had been held captive, tortured in unimaginable ways and cursed the moment he broke free of his cage. Erik thought freedom was all he wanted, that it was the best he could ever have, but something had always been missing, and now he knew what it was.

Her.

Never had he felt so alive until this moment, so desperate for his craving, so fulfilled by every second that passed by. Never had his heart beaten so fiercely, as if it had found its reason for holding on, and it was all because of her. His partner, his soul, his other half, his *mate.*

He needed to grab her, to hold her close, to roll on top of her and take her. He needed to fill her, to stop the aching desperation that was drowning him, and while he didn't know her, he knew that with absolute certainty, just as he knew she needed it too.

She'd found a way to muffle herself, but he'd heard the soft moans that left her lips when he sucked at her skin, and he felt the way her nipples hardened against his chest. He could feel his hands and arms again. He tested, lifting them, and was pleased when they moved so he could wrap his arms around her.

He pressed his body against hers, and she gasped at the contact. His hands inched up her back, until they became tangled in her leather jacket. He growled in frustration and tore it off her, laying it on the ground.

Erik wanted nothing between them and shred the offending material as he rolled her onto her back and climbed on top of her.

He ran his hands over her soft skin, felt the goose-bumps as he traced down her neck to her breasts. Erik squeezed them in his hands, rolled his thumbs over her nipples. He heard the sharp intake of her breath, and pleasure ran through him. He wanted to take his time with her, to feel her, stroke her, hear her breathless, melodic cries, but he also wanted to devour her, absorb her, to become one with her.

Erik knew he wasn't worthy of her for so many reasons. But he couldn't stop. He *ached* for her. He wasn't just hungry for her blood or her taste; he hungered for the warmth in her that staved away the emptiness in him, and he would do anything to have it, take everything she had to give, and give all of himself in return.

Her hands roamed his back, pulling him closer as she widened her legs—legs that he fit so perfectly in between. He pressed against her pussy, groaning at the barrier of his pants. She heard him, felt that frustration, and lowered her hand to the band. She fumbled with the closure, and he helped her, sending the button flying somewhere against a wall. Carefully, together, they lowered the zipper.

She took him in her hands, and he swore he saw paradise. Her touch weakened him, made him tremble as he thrust into her small hands. His beautiful mate angled her hips, planning on guiding him inside, but he grabbed her and stopped her. His fingers ran over her stomach, and he heard her breath hitch. Then he slid down, flittering over her pubic hair until he reached her clit. He wanted her to enjoy this, wanted her to know that she was his priority, even if he could barely contain himself from ramming inside her.

Her hips undiluted beneath him, circling, taking the pleasure he gave. His fingers traveled lower, trailed her pussy lips then dipped inside. She shuddered and arched at the intrusion, and he groaned in satisfaction. She was so wet, so ready for him.

"Please," she begged. "Please fuck me. I need you, Erik."

How could he deny her? How, when she said his name so beautifully, when she begged so perfectly?

Erik lifted his mouth from her neck. He licked the blood from the spot, and she shivered. He braced himself on one hand to look down at her. Her eyes were dilated, the dark olive orbs so close to black, glowing as she watched him. Her mouth was parted, each breath shorter than the last. He grasped his cock and guided it to her entrance, ran the tip between her pussy lips to coat it in her wetness, and he watched as her mouth opened wider and she moaned for him. Her eyes flickered from his face down to his cock, and she bit her lip. It made him grin, but the smile died on his face when he couldn't remember her name. He knew her in his soul, felt the love he had for her that was as deep and vast as the ocean, but his couldn't remember a single thing about her, and he refused to take her that way.

Erik opened his mouth to speak but found his throat dry at the notion of asking her a question that was sure to hurt her, even if he knew he had to. He licked his lips and finally said, "Will you tell me your name?"

Her eyes flew to his. Sadness filled her gaze, but she smiled at him regardless. "Mya."

"Mya," he said, and the name felt so right slipping off his tongue. He swallowed the weight of unknown emotions, and they wrapped around his heart and squeezed. "I'm sorry I—"

"I know you don't remember." She slid her hand to his cheek, cupping it with her palm.

"But how?"

"I know the woman who helped you erase the memories. She's safe now, but she told me what she did, that you asked her to remove your memories to protect me and my family."

He remembered Johanna, bloody and used and flayed open in so many ways that they had to stitch her back together. Erik was happy to know she was safe, to know that she was with the wonderful woman beneath him. Mya had saved his life, activating their mate bond to cure him of the curse that sapped his strength and removed the nutrients he needed from blood. And this beautiful woman, his *mate,* the person who his heart was beating so strongly for, deserved better than a rough fuck against a cave floor.

He moved to get off her, but she wrapped her legs around his hips.

"Mya—"

"No," she said even as her voice shook. "Please, no. We have spent years, *centuries* waiting for the perfect time. I swore that when I found you, we would never wait again, and I would make sure we took advantage of every moment we had together. Please," she whispered, "you left me once. Do not leave me now."

He said her name on a sigh. His fingers brushed the wetness away from her cheek, leaving a small trail of dirt on her skin. "You deserve better than this."

"What I do or don't deserve isn't important. What I want is," she said, cupping his face.

The way she looked up at him as if he was her whole world was undeniable, and his heart screamed in agreement with her. They had waited too long, too many years, and they needed to finally take the opportunity they had to be together.

He sighed again. She was dangerous because he knew with absolute certainty that he would never be able to refuse her. Erik shifted, settled the weight of his body on top of hers again, and growled, "Tell me what you want."

"You," she moaned, arching her back as he ground his pelvis against her clit.

"Then I will give you all of me, all you could ever desire. Now watch me slide my cock into you. Watch how perfectly you take me."

She whimpered at his words. Once more he trailed her entrance with his cock before he slipped the head inside. They both gasped. She arched her back and he watched her every movement: the way she swallowed, the way her hands fisted his biceps as he slid into her. His pace was excruciating slow, but a constant thrust forward, until he felt a small bit of resistance.

His eyes widened. "Mya—"

She planted her feet on the ground and lifted her hips, squeezing the walls of her pussy around him, and he couldn't resist thrusting forward. She cried out in a mix of pain and pleasure, and yet she kept pushing against him. He thrust until he was halfway inside her and had to grind his teeth to keep himself from moving or coming right there on the spot.

"You were..." he bit out, panting.

She nodded frantically, licked her lips, and then she smiled up at him brilliantly. "Yes, I was, and now I'm yours."

He snarled and gripped her hips hard as he slid out of her. "You are mine. Only mine," he said, and then he thrust into her.

Her nails bit into his back as he kept sliding deeper. She cried out his name, and the sound of it leaving her mouth only made him want to fuck her harder so he could hear it again and again. He pushed at her thighs, keeping her spread wide for him until he was fully seated and surrounded by the warmth of her pretty little cunt.

Erik pulled out and thrust back in, and then he did it again and again. The way he felt inside of her was indescribable; so deep, so strong that if he died tomorrow, he would be a happy man. But the way she said his name, squeezed him, and tried to wrap herself around him just to keep him inside her, brought him to the peak of euphoria.

Each thrust was stronger, harder, deeper, his need to never be without her mounting until it fully took him over. He needed to bury himself inside her, he needed to feel her coat his cock with her come while he shot his own within her. His feelings went beyond need, beyond desire, beyond a craving; it was pure, endless madness.

He lifted himself from her, and she wrapped her arms around him..

"Made for me," he moaned as he sat down on the floor with her in his lap.

"Yes," she hissed as he slid himself back inside of her.

He impaled her with his cock, gripped her hips and helped her ride him while he met her with every thrust. They bounced together, her breasts against his chest, her arms clinging to him as his hands ghosted her spine, squeezed her back, because he couldn't stand to be separated from her for even a moment. But it was her eyes, the way they stared into his as if they could see into his very soul, that undid him, and he knew in that very moment that no matter what, even if he had no right to her, even if she grew tired of him, even if he hurt her, even if he perished, it would always be them. They were inseparable, undeniable, inextinguishable.

He would never let her go, never let her have another. He would be whatever she wanted, do whatever she needed him to do, give her whatever she needed to keep her happy, because she had claimed him body, mind, heart, and soul, and he didn't want any of those spaces back. In fact, he wanted her to take them, to fill them, to keep them, just as much as he wanted to steal her own.

"Mine," he growled again, because he couldn't form the words he wished to when her pussy was gripping him, milking his cock.

"Yours," she cried out.

He kissed her with everything in him, trying to convey what she'd done to him, to share and show her all the ways she'd driven him completely delirious with her touch. She whimpered into his mouth, and he cupped her head. His fingers traveled to her scalp, and he gripped the long strands of her hair, keeping their lips fused together.

She moaned louder, her body shaking against his as he picked up the pace. He licked her lips and she opened immediately for his tongue. He could still taste her blood, but now he could taste her as well, the mint from her toothpaste, the coffee with cream and three sugars. He loved exploring her, finding out more about her, but now he wanted to know how she looked when she came for him.

It was that need that made him finally break from her mouth, and they both gasped, breathless and moaning. Erik rested his head against her own and whispered, "I want to watch you come, Mya. I want to see what you look like when you've lost every ounce of control. Lean back on my thighs and take my cock. Take what you need from me."

She obeyed him so eagerly, so happy to please, and leaned back on his legs, riding him with wild abandon. Her head fell back when he grabbed her breast with one hand and drew the nipple of her other in his mouth. He sucked and licked it, moaning at her taste, the feel of her, just as he thrust inside her, and every time she said his name, he grew closer and closer to filling her to the brim.

"It's too much. It's too much!" she whimpered.

He let her nipple go with a *pop*, then took control of her hips again. "Clearly it isn't if you haven't come for me."

"I need ... I *need*..." She trailed off, wrapping her arms around him, and then she latched onto his neck, sinking her fangs into his throat.

His eyes rolled back into his head, and he lost all sense of control. Every drop of blood she drank from him increased the frantic brutality of his thrusts. He was lost to sensation, lost to her, and he was never coming back.

A feeling burned deep within him, one he had not felt in eight months: his ability to create and manipulate fire. Without warning it broke free and slid up and around them, covering them in a wall of liquid warmth. The heat coated every part of their bodies, including his cock, and it caused Mya to scream his name.

Her head tossed back as he poured more of his magic into her. Her thighs shook, her eyes opened wide, she clung to him, squeezed him. If he had been a lesser man then her grip on him might have killed him, but he loved the danger of his mate being consumed by the passion between them.

And then she came, and it triggered his own release. He came so hard he lost all sense of reason, time, space. The air, the ground beneath their bodies ... None of it matter. Nothing existed but her. He continued to ram inside of her until he had filled her, and when his come leaked out of her, he pushed it back in.

CHAPTER 16

They walked along the narrow pathway to the abandoned church Erik called home in necessary silence. The church was on the outskirts of the city, hidden from most. It was rumored to be haunted, and had mostly been reclaimed by the forest, but it was still a structure, and there was no telling if Constance's vampires were still looking for him or how close they were. They needed to be quiet, to stay alert and be vigilant in using their senses to alert them of danger.

Time was of the essence, Erik knew that, but he still wished they could have stayed in that cave—in each other's arms—because the moment they separated the distance between them seemed unfathomable. Erik knew it was his fault. It was odd not remembering the person he loved the most—all the times they'd spent together, laughed together, their *history*—and yet still feeling the deep, all-consuming love he had for her. And then there was the grief, the sickness, the hurt and pain he knew he had caused Mya. He wanted to get on his knees and beg for her forgiveness. He had the need to hold her, to tell her it was all going to be okay, that he would never leave her again, and yet he didn't understand why he would have ever left her in the first place.

Missing so many of the pieces left him unsure, off-balance. It was not the first time he'd felt that way. When he'd escaped the cage, he'd felt insurmountable pain. He pushed himself through the journey, self-preservation flooding his body with adrenaline, and managed to escape the cave before everything collapsed. But as he stood outside, free, finally achieving his greatest wish, he realized there was so much he didn't know. The world had changed around him, and he had not seen it as a free man in over two hundred years. He had no idea where to go, what to do, and he had to admit he'd grown complacent.

As Constance's captive he was tortured, bled to within an inch of his life for weeks on end, castrated, branded, dismembered. His body had healed from those instances, regrowing his limbs, keeping him whole, but his mind had come to expect the routine. He lived in constant misery. Now he had hope, he had the ability to live, to feed, to breathe fresh air. It was terrifying, but he'd survived it, just as he'd survived being a punching bag for years.

And yet whatever it was he'd done to Mya caused him more pain and agony than any single one of those instances. All because he'd hurt her. But he would still approach it in the same way, using courage and dedication to push through the fear of possibly losing her. She'd asked him not to leave her, and he promised he wouldn't, but he would not let her leave him either.

He tapped her on her shoulder when it was time to turn, and they traveled over a hill and down into the valley which emptied into the small town. A few steps later, they arrived at the church. Erik guided her to the back and had her wait while he made his way inside, carefully avoiding the traps he'd laid. After reviewing them and confirming that none had been triggered, he opened the door for Mya and led her down to the basement, where the church had a tunnel that led to the other side of the cave system.

Erik lit a torch near the wall, wincing at his surroundings. He had a bed, dresser, mirror, a usable restroom considering he washed himself in the river, but his living arrangements were meager at best. Yet again he found himself not living up to what Mya deserved, and yet again he felt like a failure to her. But when he looked at her, no judgment or criticism clouded her face. Her eyes were downcast, and when he made a move toward her, a shaky breath escaped her lips.

Mya cleared her throat and said, "Do you have anything I can change into?"

They'd managed to make a covering out of the scraps of her clothes, but she needed something that would not threaten to reveal her if she moved the wrong way. He reached into the dresser and pulled out the smallest sizes of clothing he'd stolen. He looked at her, then back at the clothing in his hand and sighed. "I think these will be too big for you, but it's the best I have. I'm sorry."

"No, it's okay. This is just fine." Mya took the clothing from him and fidgeted. "Is there somewhere I can change?"

Right here, with my help.

He shook himself of the thought. "Of course. I'll go upstairs. If you need to clean up, walk this way and make a right," he said, gesturing down the tunnel. "It leads to the river. It's fast moving here, so be careful."

"I will be."

He grabbed the largest shirt he owned and a pair of pants, then he motioned to the door. "If you need help, just call for me."

She gave him a small smile and he left to dress himself upstairs. He had managed to find something that fit his new, healthy form: a black top—a wifebeater, as humans called it, although why they chose that name he would never understand—and a pair of gray sweatpants. He caught a reflection of himself and winced. After cleaning himself up, Erik took a pair of sheers to his hair, evening out the length, changed, and then he waited for Mya.

Eventually the door opened, and Mya stood shyly in front of him. For a moment he just stared at her. She took his breath away every time he looked at her, and his heart beat a little faster as need funneled through his veins.

A small smile graced her lips. Then she drew back, as if snapping out of a trance, and broke the connection between them with a shake of her head. "Do you need to grab anything before we go?"

He knew the plan. They were supposed to come here, get whatever he might need or that might be important to him, then destroy the church and go to Mya's house. From there he would meet Johanna and her partner, Luke--someone Erik apparently knew but could not remember--and restore his memories. It was a good plan, a solid plan, one that would work, but one look at Mya's face told him he couldn't take another second of not trying to broach this distance, to fix what had happened between them. Even if they had a million more important things to do, this was what mattered most—her comfort and nurturing their relationship, whatever she may allow it to be.

Erik tipped his head at the pew in front of him. "I need you to stop and tell me what I did. Tell me how I broke your heart."

Mya shook her head. "We don't have time—"

"Then we will *make* time. Sit down and talk to me, Mya. I know I'll get my memories back, but right now, I need to hear what happened from you. I need to know what you've gone through all these years."

He took a deep breath and stared into her sad eyes.

"No more distance. No more protecting my feelings or biding time. If you need to lash out at me, do it. If you need to fight me, do it. If you need to kill me, do it. But let me in, love. Let me ease your soul in whatever way I can."

———

There was so much, *too* much, when it came to them and their history.

Mya knew what would happen when she gave him her blood. She knew it would trigger the mate bond, and she did not regret a moment of their time in that cave, but once everything had ended and the sweat on her skin began to cool, reality hit her. He was there. Erik was back. Every time she opened her eyes, he was in front of her. It wasn't a dream, or a memory, or a nightmare where he would suddenly disappear into the darkness again. No matter how many times she blinked or breathed, his form never changed. He was flesh and bone, and actually real for the first time in three hundred years. The emotions it made her feel were too heavy for her to carry, especially now when she was trying to get him to safety.

For years, all she had ever wanted was to see him, to be with him again, and now that her wish had come true, she felt scared. Her anger had risen to the surface. Questions flooded her mind about where he'd been, why he'd left her, how could he have done this to them, and why couldn't he have believed in her that fateful day?

Mya knew it wasn't fair of her to think those things. He'd been held captive, and she had no idea for how long nor what he had endured. She wasn't even sure what he remembered and what he didn't. She knew she shouldn't blame him, and yet a small part of her still did.

Another part of her blamed the circumstances, that they had let fate constantly get in the way of their relationship. She refused to take that out on Erik. He didn't deserve it, and it was clear that even if he didn't remember the time they'd spent together, he did, at least, feel something for her. But how could she open her heart to him? How could she let down her guard and tell him everything that had happened both before and after he left? And how could she say it in a way that wouldn't hurt him?

Mya sat on the pew in front of him, clenching his ring. It had been a constant symbol of remembrance, a vow she'd taken to never forget him or what they'd shared, and just as it had always done in moments of uncertainty, holding the small trinket made her feel brave.

She licked her dry lips. "Do you remember your last name?"

He shook his head.

"Your name is Erik Haraldsen, and my name is Mya Novak-Haraldsen."

His eyes grew wide in shock. "We're married?"

She smiled sadly as she fiddled with his ring. "No, but we would have been. You saved me, my brother, Gregori, and my cousin, Lucas, from the Black Plague. Then you became our guardian. You taught us, trained us, and eventually you and I fell in love with one another."

She swallowed through the torrent of emotions threatening to break open her heart. "We were together in secret. You went by the name of Lord Erik Devereux in England, and that made you a target. You were concerned that if you made any enemies and they knew we were together, they would come after me—whether they were human or immortal—and because I was a young vampire, my safety would be at risk. Unfortunately, you were right."

Erik squeezed the wood of pew in his fist. His jaw clenched, but he said nothing.

"We came to America to escape the attacks on immortals in Europe, but they happened here too. We thought the blood witches were behind it, but we didn't know who they were, so you and my brother decided to form The Council to safeguard us all."

She licked her lips again and squeezed the ring so hard she had to remind herself to release it before it broke. "The day all the members agreed to form The Council, I had a horrible feeling. I told you about it that morning, but you promised it would all be okay. You reminded me why we were doing this and said that if we could just cement the idea then we would have no reason to keep our relationship a secret. You told me you wanted to marry me, that you would come back home to *me*."

Mya furiously wiped away a tear and took a shaky breath to try and calm her anger. "But you didn't. I saw you with a woman. You were fucking *her*," she spat, and had to force her rage down once again. "At first, I thought it was you, but the scent was all wrong, and I soon realized it was an imposter. I killed them and ran to where they told me you were, but I got there too late. You had been tricked in the same way I had been, but you hadn't seen through it. You thought I'd rejected you and wrote me a goodbye letter—"

Her voice cracked. Erik stood, but she raised her hand, needing to say this now, to get it out.

"You said you were going to kill yourself and you left me everything you owned. I followed your scent to the cliffs and thought you'd jumped over. Then the blood witches set your house on fire." She scraped the tears from her cheeks. "I followed them, and I killed all of them and burned their house just as they had burned yours."

She stood and stepped in between his legs. When he reached for her, she flinched, and he dropped his hands to his sides. She wanted to apologize, but she didn't know how to form the right words when she was eviscerated by emotion and vulnerable even to the sight of him, so she did the only thing she could. She continued her story.

"For years I was lost without you. I wanted to die. I tried to kill myself, but my brother didn't believe you were dead and fought for me to stay alive. I was angry at him for that, and I was so angry with you for leaving me, for not giving me a chance. I've ... managed through the years. I go out on hunts, and I kill, and it makes me feel a little bit better because whoever I save gets a second chance. I take risks because if I die it doesn't matter, and for three hundred years that's how I've lived."

"Mya—"

She shook her head, and he closed his mouth. "I lived that way until eight months ago, when I found out you were alive and were being held captive. Since that day I've been scouring the city for you. All I wanted to do was find you, and now that I have, I can't believe you're here. I'm scared you're just a ghost that will disappear if I touch you. When I think of what we did in that cave, that I gave my virginity to you, I worry that it's all just a dream, that I'm asleep somewhere right now and when I wake up, I'll have to go back to the horrible reality where you're not standing in front of me. I'm both overjoyed to see you and terrified of losing you every single second that goes by. I've never felt so weak and so scared in my whole life, Erik."

She forced herself to breathe to try to stop the way her body trembled from that fear. "When you left, you took me with you, and now that you're back, I'm forced to reflect on things I never thought I would. I don't want to be distant from you, but I don't want to hurt you with my anger and hostility. I want to love you, but I'm afraid that when you get your memories back and I find out you left me because I was never enough to keep you, it will damage me beyond repair. And even with all of that I want to hope…"

Mya trailed off. She struggled as she took off the necklace and undid the clasp, pulling the ring free and letting the chain drop to the floor. "But it doesn't matter, does it? Because in the end, regardless of what happened, of how many years have gone by, there's only one thing that will always be the truth between us. That I"—she took his hand and slid the ring onto his finger —"much like this ring, will always be yours."

She bit her lip hard and let the small sliver of pain cut through the sadness threatening to take her over. Then she smiled and began to walk away, to hope she could save herself from the torrent of feelings washing through her.

An arm around her waist and stopped her.

"Let me go," she said firmly.

Erik's grip tightened. "No."

"Let me go!" she screamed. "Let me go, let me go, let me go!"

She fought against his embrace, but he just held her. She couldn't break away, and she would have fallen to her knees, defeated, if he hadn't kept her close. He turned her and she sobbed into his chest so hard that she shook them both. He combed his fingers through her hair, and it made her cry even harder, because he'd always loved to do that so she'd kept her hair long in memory of him. Everything she'd done was in his memory, and now he was here. She didn't want to lose him again, didn't want to let him go, didn't want to push him away, but she was torn apart, and her mind told her that she needed to preserve herself, that distance was protection.

"I'm sorry," he whispered into her hair while he stroked her back. "I'm so sorry."

She continued to sob, her tears hot and angry as the pain she'd felt for centuries poured out of her. When at last her grief began to lessen, he squeezed her shoulders.

"I didn't leave you," he said, his voice so strong and sure, but Mya knew he was mistaken.

"You did."

"No, I didn't."

She drew away from him and furiously wiped her face with the back of her hands. "Please don't say that for my benefit. Don't lie to me."

"Mya," he whispered, and the way he said her name like a tormented plea made her pause. He cupped her face and made her look up at him as he said again, "I did not leave you. I swear it."

"And the letter telling me goodbye? What was that then?"

"I don't know—"

She shook her head and tried to pull back from him, but he held her still.

"Stop."

It was not a suggestion but a command, and even after all this time she found herself pathetically listening to it.

"What you said, what happened to you..." He swallowed. "What I *made* happen to you broke my heart, but when you turned to walk away, to hide yourself from me? It shattered me, Mya. I cannot fathom not having you by my side, and I cannot think about not being by yours."

She dropped her eyes from his. "Because we consummated our mate bond."

"No!" he said sharply, and her eyes snapped to his. "No," he said again, running his fingers over her cheeks. "When Johanna takes your memories, it feels like something's missing. It's in the back of your mind but you can't figure out what it is, and your heart can't connect to it. I knew there was something I wanted to get to, something I searched for beyond freedom, but I didn't know what it was or where to find it. I didn't know, until you saved me."

She turned her head from his, but he ever so gently, so carefully pulled it back. She closed her eyes, guarding herself from his expression because she couldn't stand to see the way he begged her to believe him. If she did, if she looked at him now, she would. She'd believe anything he told her, trust his decisiveness, his devotion, as she always had, and in the end, it would only break her further when his memories came back and the truth was revealed.

His lips brushed her eyelids in a gentle kiss that stole her breath. "You are my salvation, Mya. I knew it from the moment I laid eyes on you, just as I know what my heart felt then and what it feels now. There are a lot of things there—despair, concern, sorrow—but there are other things too. Hope. Patience. Compassion. But more than anything, love. I love you. I loved you, and I will always love you, even if you were to leave me today. But if you did, you would take my heart and the entire essence of who I am. I know that now, and I know I knew that before, just like I know it would have been the same way for you. I would have never willingly, *selfishly*, put you through that pain. And when I get my memories back, I will prove it to you. I swear it."

CHAPTER 17

Mya's house was deceiving. It sat toward the back of a large, encased piece of land, lined by trees and the lush forest on either side. It was entirely made of stone in a cottage style, but the real brilliance was the interior.

Erik was struck by the space the moment he entered the front door. Several of the walls were lined with large sets of seamless glass doors that led to an open court-yard with trees, hedges, a circular fountain, and flowers. He had never seen anything like it.

Mya locked the door behind him and followed his line of sight. "I like to be alone, so I prefer to spend most of my time here. It's easier when you have a view like this and can bring the outdoors into your home."

"It's beautiful," Erik said, staring right at her.

She blushed, twirling her fingers for a moment before she said, "My cell phone is in my bedroom. I'll call Johanna and let her know we're here. Feel free to take a look around."

She went to move past him, but he grabbed her hands and brought them to his lips. "Thank you for inviting me into your home and sharing your space with me."

His grin grew wider when she blushed again, and with a nod she hurried past him.

Erik ventured deeper into the house. There weren't any personal photos of Mya or her family. Instead, the shelves were covered with plants, books on different subjects, old worn journals, and small trinkets.

He moved to the second floor, where most of the doors were open except for one. Behind it he could smell something burning. Erik pondered for a moment, not wanting to intrude, but also concerned for her property. When he finally decided to open the door, he was shocked by what he saw.

Several tall red candles were lit, giving off a smell of cinnamon and something else he couldn't put a name to. Above the candles was a portrait, and it was like he was looking into a mirror.

"Erik..."

He jumped back and took in the horror etched on her face. "Mya, I'm sorry. I thought—"

She bit her lip and shook her head. Then she cleared her throat. "No, it's okay. It's my fault. I forgot."

He left the room, closed the door gently, and moved toward her. She hugged herself as if to keep her distance from him, but he refused to let her shy away. Instead, he pulled her to his chest. "I'm sorry," he whispered.

Her hands dropped, and after a moment she wrapped her arms around him and breathed him in while she pushed her head further into his chest.

"It's my way of making sure I always remember you. Every night I light the candles. I change them throughout the day to make sure they're always burning. I used to talk to you ... to your picture, I mean. I'd tell you how much I loved you, how much I missed you. That I hoped you were somewhere safe, born into a better life where you could be happy, and maybe one day I'd get to see you again."

He tilted her face to his. "And now you can."

She nodded and bit her lip. "Now I can."

"Mya..." His gaze roamed hers before settling on her lips. "May I kiss you?"

She gripped his shirt. "Johanna will be here in a couple of minutes and—"

"Just one kiss, please."

Her eyelids closed as she angled her head to his, and he descended slowly, wanting her to know that she could pull away at any time.

"I need to hear it, Mya," he whispered against her lips.

"Yes," she whispered.

He kissed her, and it was as if light had flooded his heart when her lips moved against his. He gathered her closer, and she wrapped her arms around him. It was a kiss of gentle completion, of love and sadness, of hope and despair. It was a kiss that began their path to healing the wound that had been infected and festering for years between them.

Erik pulled away from her soft mouth slowly, then kissed her forehead before running his fingers over her cheek and down her hair. "Thank you for giving me something so precious."

Her eyes opened slowly, and they were so vulnerable his heart skipped a beat. "What have I given you?"

"Your time. Your mind. Your energy. Your love. They are all of the highest value. Priceless," he said, staring into her eyes, "and I will spend the rest of my life appreciating them and you."

Before she could say anything in response, another presence filled the air. Erik growled low in his throat, and pushed Mya behind him, but she gripped his arm.

"It's okay, Erik. It's just Johanna and Luke."

Erik locked his eyes onto hers. His brow furrowed. "But they didn't come through a door."

She smiled at him. "They don't need to. Come on."

Mya led him downstairs to the living room, where he saw a tall man with golden skin and short brown hair whose mouth dropped open when his green-gray eyes landed on Erik. Several different emotions ran over his face, and Erik wished he remembered him, wished he knew who the man was.

Then his eyes moved to Johanna, and he grinned.

Her long blonde hair was shiny, her eyes a vibrant blue glistening like the ocean, and she was no longer marred in cuts and bruises. She looked well taken care of, nourished, and exuded a type of peace that he had never seen from her. There was more there, under the surface, but she was thriving, and it was evident in every single way.

"Erik!" she shouted, running to him and tossing her arms around him. He caught her, laughing as he swung her around before setting her down on the floor. She laughed with him, tears rolling down her cheeks when she cupped his face. "I knew you were alive! I knew it, but it still doesn't seem real!"

He grabbed her arms and pulled back to look at her. "And you as well. You look happy, Johanna, and so incredibly loved. You deserve that."

His eyes slid to man, and Erik realized he must be Luke. For a moment something flickered in his memory. The figures were shadowed. They had no faces, made no gestures or actions, but he could feel the man's loneliness, the void he'd carried inside that he constantly tried to keep at bay. And yet, as Erik looked at Luke now, that void was gone.

"You deserve that too," Erik said.

Luke blinked, uncertain as to how to deal with him, but gave him a small smile. "Thank you."

"You're welcome."

Erik looked for Mya and found her leaning against a console table, her arms crossed. She was trying to appear indifferent, but he could see the jealousy on her face, the uncertainty, and when they locked eyes, she quickly looked away.

Erik turned back to Johanna. "Could you please restore my memories? I have a lifetime of mistakes to make up for with my mate."

Mya's eyes snapped to his, and he gave her a soft smile. "And I'd say with her family, too."

Johanna nodded and gestured to a chair. "Of course. You should sit, though. I took a lot from you, and it will be difficult on your mind to get all the memories back at once."

Erik took a seat, as did Luke and Mya, and then he waited. The fear that coursed through his veins at the thought of getting his memories back made him feel weak. There was time missing between Mya's story and the days of his capture. He didn't know what lie dormant there, but it felt dark, depressive.

He was still certain that he did not leave Mya's side willingly, but in the end it didn't matter. Nothing mattered except her. He had to fix this, all of it—the awkwardness, the distance, the grief and despair. He wasn't foolish enough to believe it could be resolved overnight, or even within a few years, but he wouldn't stop trying until it did. They needed that. They deserved that, and Erik knew Mya needed to see him fight for her, for them. He would fight tooth and nail, and he would conquer every single one of his demons to keep her in his life.

Johanna lifted her fingertips to his temples. He felt heavy, weighed down under a humid fog that filled the room. He struggled under it, trying to catch his breath.

And then it happened.

Mya. Gregori. Lucas. He could see their faces as clear as day. He saw them running, playing, climbing, training, fighting. He felt Mya, their first touch, first embrace. He felt the desperation, the hope that welled inside of him when he confessed his past to her, and he felt her love wash over him. He felt the rolling sea as they traveled to America. He felt the overwhelming joy of finally being able to marry her, to know that she would be protected, and then he felt the betrayal and heartache of being rejected. He felt the death of his heart and the complete obliteration of realizing it had all been a trap. He felt the worms that crawled over his skin and the way he'd sat frozen, wishing he could go to Mya when he heard her screams. And then he felt empty, broken, defeated, reduced to nothing as time passed by, until he saw the sky again and was taken captive by Constance.

When Erik came to, he was on the floor of Mya's living room. The light was too bright, the faces of those peering down at him blurry. He closed and opened his eyes multiple times before he could clearly see, and the first face that came into his vision was the one he'd always wished for, the one he missed most, the only one his heart had ever and would ever beat for.

Mya.

He reached for her, sat up and hugged her. He clung to her tightly and swore that nothing would ever separate them again. Johanna and Luke moved to help him, but he gathered them in his arms just as the tears gathered in his eyes.

———

They said their goodbyes, and Mya and Erik watched as Johanna teleported away with Luke. But even such a marvel didn't distract Erik from what he had to do next.

Mya was hurting and so was he, but they needed this conversation for him to right his wrongs, for healing to begin.

"Mya?" he started.

She looked up at him, and for a moment he couldn't speak. He was lost in the deep, wild forest that lived in her eyes, mesmerized by the shades of green yellowed by sunlight that danced every time she blinked. They were so magical, so majestic, and he had never thought he'd see them again.

He licked his lips and bared his heart to her.

"I used to dream of your eyes. I dreamed of them for years when I was alone."

His voice sounded haunted, even to his own ears, but he swallowed the feeling. He sat down on the couch, gesturing for her to join him. "Sometimes I wondered if I forgot a shade or hue. Were they darker, lighter, more golden, greener? That was…"

He licked his lips, his throat dry, and swallowed again. "That was the most terrifying part of everything —knowing how many years had gone by and wondering if I had forgotten something about you. But I never truly forgot them. For years, I would stare at the trees when we would transfer locations. I did the same after I escaped. I'd walk through the forest aimlessly. It would feel like something was crushing my heart into pieces, but I didn't know what it was."

He drew in a deep breath. "It was you, love. I was always searching for you, always hoping to find you."

Tears clouded her beautiful eyes, and she choked out his name.

"May I hold you? I know I have no right to ask but—"

"Always, *please*," she croaked and all but jumped into his lap.

He wrapped his arms around her, cradling her to him as he'd done many times when they were together. She fit so perfectly, and he missed her, a type of desolation that he had no name for. He felt her hopelessness as strongly as he felt his own. They'd survived years without one another, but they hadn't lived since the last time they touched, and he mourned all the time he lost with her.

"I'm sorry," he whispered into her hair while he ran his fingers through the silky strands, realizing how much he'd missed that too. "Your hair had become a vice for me. Without it I would fidget endlessly in that church, and nothing would sate that need. Now I know why."

She whimpered into his shoulder and squeezed her arms around his neck, clinging to him.

He kissed her head, her temple, her cheek, her neck, and she tilted for him, opened herself to him. She gave him access, gave him permission, and though he longed to take it, he couldn't until he gave her the answers she needed. She'd told him she thought she wasn't enough to keep him with her, to make him believe in their love, when that could not be further from the truth.

"I have made you cry so many tears for me, my sweet *fagr skjaldmær min,* my beautiful warrior. I do not want to make you cry anymore, but I need to tell you what happened."

She pulled back to look at him, then cupped his cheek, her warmth seeping into his skin as she smiled sadly. "It's okay. We need this."

He kissed her hand. "We do," he said, and took a deep breath. "The day we received the final approval for The Council, I told Greg I needed to get something for you. It was a ring ... an engagement ring."

Her eyes widened and a small gasp escaped her lips.

"I was going to ask you to marry me, immediately. I didn't want to wait another second. I'd been planning to for months. I had the perfect stone picked out, and the jeweler had finally finished crafting the ring. It was as if everything had perfectly aligned." He cupped her cheek, tucking her hair behind her ear. "I couldn't wait to get back to you, but on the way there…"

He trailed off as the image of her with that man flooded his memory, taking him back to the nightmare of his past. His whole body shook until Mya brought him back with a soft squeeze of his cheeks.

"I know," she whispered.

He closed his eyes, took several deep breaths to calm and refocus himself. When he spoke, his voice cracked. "I was devastated. You were, and still are, my every-thing, and believing I had lost you destroyed me. I kept walking, and I suddenly found myself in front of the house I'd built for us. I knew I couldn't live there. Every-where I looked, I saw you, because that's how I'd built the house. Every room, every finish, it was all for you."

Erik swallowed. "I wrote the letter. I gathered all the documents, and then I left the house and walked along the cliff. I felt empty. Your ring was still in my pocket. I thought about throwing it over, but I couldn't. I couldn't let you go."

He cupped her cheeks, lifted her head to his and stared into her eyes. "I. Couldn't. Let. You. Go."

She bit her lip, and he ran his thumb over it, pulling it from her teeth. "I didn't leave you. I was going to go back to the tavern to see if there was some way to reclaim your heart, but I didn't get the chance. The blood witches had finished their ritual by then, and I was too late."

Mya clung to him and squeezed his shoulders as they trembled together.

"That's why they tricked us, *fagr skjaldmær min*. They needed a way into our minds. We had never ingested their blood and were so careful about what we ate and how we fed, so they used grief and heartbreak instead. The emotions gave them a way to control us…" He looked down. "A way to control me. Your ability to heal made your blood, mind, and heart stronger. Their magic did not affect you. Since I had your blood in my system, I was able to break free of their spell, but not before most of the damage had already been done."

He closed his eyes to shake off the feeling of weakness, the darkness that plagued him. "They casted a paralysis spell on me. The only reason they didn't kill me was because I was the closest to an elder vampire they'd ever gotten their hands on. Their spell removed my ability to use any of my powers once they forced their blood inside of me. Then they buried me alive in the same spot you went to."

Mya's eyes were full of horror, her skin now ashen and pale.

"I heard you scream. You were right above me, but I couldn't get to you. I smelled the smoke of the house burning. I listened as the world changed, and all I wanted was to get back to you, but I failed. I failed you. One hundred years went by underneath that soil, and the next time I saw the sun was when Constance made me her slave. I'm sorry, *fagr skjaldmær min*. I'm so sorry I wasn't strong enough," he whispered and shook his head to clear it from the memories of his captivity.

Mya's eyes suddenly hardened. A fire lit in them, and her nails pressed into his back as she squeezed him to her, making him hiss.

"Mya?"

"Finish the story," she commanded.

He smiled at her gently, sadly. "There are some things you don't need to know, *fagr skjaldmær min*."

"No. You have had to carry your burdens for years. You asked me to tell you what happened to me, and I did. I told you everything, in full detail, even the things I regret, the things I am not proud of. I want to know everything that happened to you."

"Mya—"

"*Everything*, Erik. I will not let you carry that weight by yourself. Talk to me, just like you asked me to talk to you. Please, my love."

He took in her face, the fight in her eyes, the softness of her cheeks, the decadence of her mouth, and found his thumb rubbing along its softness. Her mouth opened for him, and he sighed.

"*Will you still want me when you know what happened?*"

He didn't realize he'd spoken aloud until she answered, "Nothing could ever stop me from wanting you. I won't look at you differently, Erik. I promise you."

He tilted her head and kissed her forehead because

he couldn't muster the courage to look her in the eye. "Constance is a blood witch."

"*Impossible*," she hissed. "I killed them all."

"She is one. I'm not sure if she was born one, found a grimoire, or obtained their spells and rituals some other way, but she is a blood witch. Her goal is children. She's obsessed with having a family, with having immortal children who are strong and powerful."

Mya drew back. "Erik, did you—"

"No!" he shouted, the simple thought of touching anyone other than Mya, disgusting to him. "No, I never touched her. She tried to get me to father a child with her, but I could not. I couldn't even get hard for her, so she tried to break our mate bond."

Mya's mouth dropped open, frozen, speechless.

"She couldn't because I'd already met you. I was already in love with you, and that emotion was too strong for the spell to work, so she took delight in torturing me instead. She..."

He forced another deep breath through his body. It was easier to think the thoughts himself than say them to her, to possibly face her judgment. He didn't want her to see how weak he had been in those moments. But Mya didn't speak or push for more. She waited patiently for him, and that gave him the courage to continue.

"She castrated me," he said in a barely audible whisper. "Multiple times."

Erik couldn't look at her, embarrassed by the trauma he'd endured. "I don't know if it's because your blood was in my system for so long or because of the paralysis spell, but I received the ability to adapt to wounds and pain. I heal faster, and once an injury has happened to my body, it takes longer for the same wound to manifest again. One strike of a sword took off my cock or my arm or my foot. In a week it would grow back. She would go to strike me again, but it would take two, three, four times before she could get through the bone, and instead of it taking a week to grow back it would take three days, two, a few hours at most."

"When that stopped working, she tried other things —fire, branding, sodomy. I was a toy for her to play with, and later an experiment. She drained me of my blood and kept me in a barely alive state while she tried to manifest my ability in her other vampires, but it never worked. When the cave system began to collapse and I escaped, she cursed me with the inability to retain the nutrients I need from blood to heal. That's why you found me the way you did. Your blood cured me and—"

He felt a tremor. At first, Erik thought that he was the one trembling, so he pushed on and on. He rushed through his story as to not get lost in it, so he could be honest and open with Mya, to give her the things she'd asked to know. If he said all the horrible things just this once, perhaps he'd never have to say them again, never have think of them again. Perhaps he could lock those memories in the past with so many other things he wished he could be rid of.

But he was not the one trembling. Mya was.

Erik marveled at the expression on her face. The rage and anger he expected was in her eyes, but there was so much more in them too. For a moment, he was scared she would pity him, that she would see him as less of a man, a coward, not the man she knew or had looked up to all those years ago. But her green orbs showed empathy, compassion, and a type of misery that matched the deepest depths of his soul.

"I'm sorry," she whimpered. "I'm so sorry, Erik. I'm so sorry."

She hugged him, squeezed him, molded her body to his own as if she could hold him back from all the demons that had dug their claws into him, and in that moment he wished she could. She cried for him, wailed and sobbed and screamed for the pain he'd experienced, and he held her just as tightly. In every sound, expression, and movement she broke another barrier in his mind and soul.

Erik clung to her. He let her take his turmoil, his darkness, and expunge it in a way he did not know how to do. He let her tears be the gateway to his own, and for the first time he realized that they did not only need to heal the trauma that had happened between them, but the trauma that was present in themselves as well.

CHAPTER 18

They talked throughout the night, wanting to reconnect, to fill in the spaces between the people they were three hundred years ago and who they were today.

Erik felt incredibly lucky and thankful to be by Mya's side again. She'd overwhelmed him with not only her care now, but the things she'd done to keep his memory alive over the centuries, not only emotionally, but logically and financially. Mya had worked with her family and Lily to forge the documentation that had burned in his house. By doing so, Mya had gained access to his savings and the insurance policy. She'd filed a claim and received the payment for his home, and allocated the money into a mirage of accounts, including high yield savings accounts, certificates of deposits, bonds and stocks. She'd even allocated him a 401K through her family's company when it was first established. The result of her efforts made him one of the wealthiest men in the world. If he wanted to buy an island, even build and monopolize one, he could and would still have money to spare. She'd also found the name of the family member he'd harmed when his blood rage was out of control and had continued to pay the man's descendants.

Mya had done anything and everything to honor him. That was her love for him, and Erik felt guilty for ever questioning it. He'd always believed he didn't deserve her, that she could and should do better, but she didn't want anything else but him. It was time he accepted and respected that. One conversation would not resolve the years of heartache they'd been through, but he was grateful for the chance to try again with her.

As the night went on, they moved to her bedroom where they could lie in one another's arms, at some point his eyes closed, and he was surprised to see the sun when he opened them again. It had been years since he'd last slept, and he knew it had only been possible because of her, because of the peace she gave his soul.

Her phone vibrated again, and she grumbled as she rolled over to answer it. She read the message and sighed. "It's my brother. He wants us to come over. Are you ready to see him?"

Greg had been Erik's closest friend, someone he trusted and enjoyed mentoring, but he was also Mya's older brother, and Erik had hurt her. He wasn't sure how Greg would react to him, whether it would be with open arms, a stoic expression, or a punch to his jaw. But regardless of what might happen, Erik wanted to see him, to begin mending that bridge as well, so he nodded.

They dressed and moved downstairs, but as Mya went to open the door, Erik pulled her behind him. Stepping forward, he grasped the doorknob in his hand and flung the door open, where they were greeted by twenty-five men on her property, seven cars, and eight more driving up the road.

Mya pulled out her knife, and Erik saw pure fury and murder in her eyes.

"No, love," he said softly, "You've fought more than enough battles for me. Let me fight this one for you."

A growl tumbled out of her chest, and he chuckled at her fierceness. The dragon's nest had been disturbed, and his beautiful warrior was ready and willing to massacre anyone who trespassed on her land or threatened him. Erik had never found her to be more perfect than in that moment.

She opened her mouth to say something, but he grasped her chin, bent down to her height, and kissed her. When he finally pulled away as their adversaries grew closer, she grasped his shirt.

"You get five seconds. *Five*," she warned. "And I'm only giving them to you because I feel like you need this. If they're not dead by then, I will be out of this door with you."

"And I will throw you over my shoulder and spank that beautiful ass of yours," he said with a grin.

She batted her eyelashes at him and said, "Careful. I might like that."

He trailed his fingers over her cheek and down her neck, where he grasped her throat, making her gasp. "You have to learn to stop teasing me, especially during a fight." He held out his hand for a weapon and she gave him a dagger, handle side first.

"Not in this lifetime or the next, my love. Now go. Five."

He rolled his eyes at her and chuckled again, then took a step out of the door. His eyes narrowed as he faced Constance's army, and his annoyance grew. They had no right to be here on Mya's property, to sully her soil with even a single one of their footprints. But there was another question that he had to ask: How had they found them? Her house was far enough away that they shouldn't have been able to track them, unless there was something in him that had led them there.

He bared his teeth. The rogues moved, but they were not fast enough. Erik was an elder, and with his strength and powers restored, a small army would be nothing to him. He used the sun's rays to superpower his fire ability, and those that were hit disintegrated immediately. Then he threw balls of burning fire at the cars, exploding those nearest to them. For the few that were still alive, he dashed toward them and stabbed them clean through their brains, killing them all before the first body had even dropped to the ground.

He walked back to Mya and wiped the blood from the dagger on his pants. She greeted him at the front door, dragging his face to hers. He picked her up and crushed his lips to hers. Kissing Mya was like coming home, like finding peace and sanctuary. It was passionate, wanton. It was *right*.

"You were cutting it close," she whispered, her tone low and husky when they separated, and his heart beat a little faster at the sound.

"I'll make sure to kill them faster next time, my queen." He nuzzled her neck and put her down before they turned back to the scene. "Mya—"

"I know. I'm calling a cleaning crew and letting Greg know what happened. He has a lot of contacts. Maybe one of them can figure out how they found us."

———

Walking through Greg's house brought back a lot of memories for Erik. The vase displayed in the alcove was from a dig they'd joined in Spain, another trinket on a shelf was from an Indian man they'd saved in England, and there were several other pieces from the time they'd spent together over the centuries.

Erik didn't know it at the time but saving Greg had opened the door to his happiest memories. It had given him the family he'd lost so many years ago, and he hoped he could reclaim a piece of that family again.

When he walked into Greg's kitchen and found him cooking with his wife and mate, Daniella, Erik was struck by how much he had changed. The Gregori he knew had only ever been focused on taking care of others. He'd been the brains of their operation, a leader in his own right, far better at it than Erik. But he had never, ever seemed so relaxed, so carefree, so jovial. It made Erik immediately like Daniella and the effect she had on him, and he liked her even more when she gave Mya the tightest hug and he saw the smile that lit up her face. She meant something to Mya, and Erik was happy to see her friends, her family, people who she could share her heart with.

Then Daniella came over to him, and he could feel her assessing him in her mind before she threw open her arms to hug him. "It's nice to finally meet you, Erik. I've heard a lot about you."

"You too," he said as he hugged her back.

Greg lifted a tray of hors d'oeuvres out of the oven. As if it was a sign, Daniella grabbed Mya's arm and began to pull her of the kitchen.

"W-What are you doing?" she asked, laughing as she stumbled along with her friend.

"Giving the boys their privacy. Come say goodbye to Ruby before Elaine takes her for the night, and catch me up on all the details," Daniella said, winking at Greg before leaving them alone.

Erik waited patiently as Greg moved around the kitchen. He gave Erik a single look, but otherwise didn't acknowledge him as he mixed a batch of items together and put another tray in the oven.

It wasn't that Erik was afraid of Greg. It was a matter of respect. If the tables were turned and Greg had hurt someone Erik loved, especially a sibling, Erik wasn't sure what he would feel if he saw him again. Greg was the reason Mya was still here today. He had stopped her from taking her life multiple times, and while Mya now knew Erik never left her, Greg did not.

"It's been a long time, old friend," Erik said finally.

Greg sighed and turned to him. "It has been. It's good to see you."

Erik's eyes widened. "Really?"

Greg nodded. "I wasn't sure how I'd feel seeing you standing in front of me. I thought I'd be angry."

"You'd have every right to be."

"Perhaps, but I never believed you had actually left Mya. Am I right about that?"

Erik's jaw ticked at the thought and he nodded. "You are. I would never leave her. She's my everything."

"Then there isn't a reason for me to be angry."

Greg grabbed several dirty dishes and brought them to the sink. Erik followed suit, grabbing the remaining items and bringing them to Greg, who smiled in thanks.

"You don't want to know what happened? You don't … need me to tell you?"

"No."

For the second time in less than five minutes, Greg had shocked him.

"You've always been brooding. Quiet. Stoic, even, but now you're unsure," Greg said, and Erik averted his gaze. "I don't mean that in an embarrassing way. I just mean that it's clear to me you've been through a lot, and it isn't just that you've been missing for so many years."

Greg turned away from the sink and leaned back against it. "I know trying to get your bearings after so long is going to be difficult, and I'm certain you weren't being fed expensive cheese and wine during your time with Constance. You've gone through enough, and honestly, I'm just happy to have you back."

Greg looked toward the door and Erik followed his line of sight, watching Mya talk to Daniella, Luke, and Johanna. She was smiling, laughing, and it filled his heart with joy.

"I haven't seen her like that since before you ... since you've been gone. She'll laugh, and she'll smile, but it's—"

"Weighed down," Erik answered, remembering the smile she gave him at the church before they'd spoken.

Greg looked at him then, his gaze hard. "You took that smile off her face when you left, and you've brought it back now that you're here. I need you to fight for her, Erik, for the *both* of you, because you deserve it." He crossed his arms and glared at him. "If you leave again, you better stay gone or else I will kill you myself."

Erik's gaze never wavered from Greg's as he said, "I'd do it myself if I left her."

"Then we have an understanding. Come here." Greg stepped forward and gave him a hug with a pat on his back.

Erik returned the embrace and couldn't help but smile. "Thank you."

"Of course. And I called some friends who wanted to see you."

Erik tilted his head to the side, "Who—"

"Well, if you're not a sight for sore eyes."

He turned to see Lily coming through the door. She had a huge smile on her face that crinkled her eyelids, and he laughed while he gave her a tight hug. She gave his arms a squeeze, then stepped back and rested her hands on the shoulders of a woman who had appeared beside her. "Erik, I'd like to introduce you to my wife, Oaklynn."

Oaklynn was short—likely under five feet tall—with long reddish-brown hair and brown eyes. She reminded Erik of a firecracker, and he knew immediately that she was Lily's perfect match.

"It's nice to meet you," she said, holding out her hand, which Erik shook.

"You as well."

Greg gave Lily and Oaklynn a hug in greeting as well. "Technically they're not supposed to be here since Lily is still part of The Council, and that makes it a conflict of interest but—"

"We couldn't stay away once we found out you were alive," Oaklynn said with a smile.

"You've been missed, Erik," Lily said, her expression softening as her eyes began to glisten.

Daniella poked her head around the door frame, and Greg clapped his hand on Erik's shoulder. "Well, now that we're all here it's time for us to get started."

———

Erik shared everything he knew thus far, including that Constance's army had found him at Mya's house earlier that day.

"Have they ever found you so easily before?" Merida asked, one of Greg's seconds-in-command.

"Yes, but I thought it was something I had done. Clothing, where I was staying wasn't secure enough, and so on," Erik said.

Mya laced her fingers through his. "But that wasn't the case with my house. We burned the church, got rid of anything Erik had before except for the clothes he has on now, and if they had some sort of tracking device on those—"

"Then they would have grabbed him then, not waited for you to come along," Greg finished.

Mya nodded.

"It could be a magical locator spell. Have you ever ingested Constance's blood?" Oaklynn asked.

Erik grimaced, then nodded.

"That would be enough." Oaklynn fished for her bag, and pulled out an old leather book, crackling with power.

Luke's eyes grew wide. "Is that…"

"Yes," Oaklynn said with a nod. "It's a blood witch grimoire. Not all of us are evil." Her eyes touched every person in the room as her words hung in the air.

"Oaklynn is the reason we were able to create blood banks and extract platelets that specifically aid vampires. She's a pathologist, as well as a blood witch." Lily said, as she squeezed Oaklynn's leg and smiled at her with pride.

"I know blood witches have caused immortals a lot of heartache over the centuries, but there's more than just one side to us. Our abilities can heal, and we can do a lot of good. The blood witches you've met were turned to the magic, not naturally born, and that turning makes them crazy. Much like a rogue vampire."

"What does that mean?" Johanna asked.

"Essentially, the magic those blood witches use is a type of curse. It can only be triggered by extreme trauma and will quite, literally drive them crazy. There's no saving them from that madness. They will fixate on one specific theme, likely what caused them to gain access to that magic in the first place, and they will continue down that path until they die."

Oaklynn turned another page from the grimoire. "I'm not saying that because I sympathize with them. What they've done is inexcusable and they deserve to die but knowing what they're fixated on may help us to better understand why they've done what they've done. Once we know that, we might know how to stop them."

"Children."

Everyone's gaze shifted to Erik, and Mya squeezed his hand, anchoring him to the present and keeping his mind from slipping into the past.

"Constance's focus is on children," he said.

"Could she have lost a child?" Merida asked.

Oaklynn leaned back against the couch, flicking through the pages of the book. "If that's the case she's going to want to make more, and fast. She'd capture powerful immortals to father her new children."

"But we've never found any children at any of the places we've infiltrated," Greg said, crossing his arms.

"Maybe children are too difficult for her," Daniella said, drawing their gaze. "Maybe she wants children, but she can't be a mother, and that's why she's kidnapped and turned so many humans so she can have the family she's always wanted without having to raise them."

"It would explain why she's so focused on making them stronger," Erik said, and several of their group nodded in agreement.

"That would also explain why she's focused on you. You're the current key to her strengthening her family," Merida said, her expression apologetic.

Erik could feel Mya's annoyance rising at the

thought, so he squeezed her hand and then wrapped his arm around her shoulders.

"I've found the locator spell," Oaklynn said, looking up from the book. "It's not a permanent solution for her. She can only use it for as long as she has your blood and for as long as you have hers in your system. Mya said that you were under a curse when she found you?"

"Yes," Erik said. "It kept me from absorbing the nutrients we need in blood and stopped me from using my powers."

Oaklynn made a soft humming sound. "I have an idea of what she did to you. That spell, even after being broken, lasts for three days. That's the connection she has with you. Her magic is still in your blood, and that's what she's using to power the locator spell."

"Which means she's going to come after me with everything she can," Erik said, and Oaklynn nodded.

Erik watched as Greg and Daniella shared a look. It told him that they had a plan, and he wasn't going to like it.

Greg cleared his throat. "Then we need to use that while we still can."

Mya's head snapped and she glared at her brother. "What are you saying, Gregori?"

"Mya," he said softly, "we have the opportunity to catch her right in front of us." His gaze moved to Erik. "We need to discuss taking it."

"*What* are you saying," she bit out again.

"We may need to use Erik as bait."

"No!" She rushed to her feet. "How could you even suggest that? Erik…" She stared at him, a look of horror crossing her face. "You … Tell me you don't agree with this."

"My love—" He reached for her, but she smacked his hands away.

"I just got you back. I *just* got you back after so long. How could you? How could you want to do this when I may never see you again?"

"Mya, please—"

"No!" she screeched, and before he could move, she ran from the room.

CHAPTER 19

Mya felt Erik's presence from the hallway. She wished she could stand to be away from him, but she couldn't.

When he opened the door, all she could mutter was a weak, "Leave me alone," even while her body begged for his touch, for him to sweep her into his arms and promise he wasn't leaving.

Erik closed the door gently behind him. She could feel him at her back, and when he wrapped his arms around her, she sunk into his warmth as though he had pulled her out of the freezing cold.

His tone was so soft, so broken as he said, "*Fagr skjaldmær min*, please don't run away from me. It breaks my heart to watch you walk away, or for you to tell me to leave you. I will never leave you. I promised I wouldn't."

The thought of him leaving cut through her like a knife of betrayal, and she spun out of his embrace.

"That's right, you promised, but that's exactly what you're wanting me to watch you do, leave."

"My love—"

"Would you be okay if it was me? Would you be fine with letting me go out there and be the *bait?*" she snapped, fully knowing the answer.

His eyes narrowed and filled with fury.

"That's what I thought."

Erik took a deep breath, then tilted her chin up to his. "You're right, *fagr skjaldmær min,* but there's a difference between you and me. You do not have a locator spell that turns you into a giant beacon for the enemy."

She bit her lip.

"My love, I dealt with them easily today, but that wasn't even a quarter of Constance's army. Who knows how much they've grown since I've been free. You heard Oaklynn. They had three days to find me. One day has already passed. They could find me *anywhere*: at your house, here. What happens if Greg and Daniella are here alone with Ruby?"

Mya shook her head, but the image of Greg and Dani fighting, of any possible danger coming to her niece, was still there. She averted her eyes from Erik's and tried to steady her tone even though she felt like she was drowning. "Th-They could handle it. We could plan for it."

Erik stroked her cheek, drawing her gaze. "Gregori is the same age I was when they buried me alive. I believe in him and his wife's abilities, but when they would also have to protect their child ... It's selfish to put them through that, and you, my love, have never been selfish."

Mya's knees shook at the thought of losing her brother, or Dani and Ruby, but her heart was breaking at the thought of losing Erik again, of something going wrong, of him truly dying this time.

"I don't want to lose you," she whispered.

"You won't," he said as he tucked her hair behind her ear.

"How do you know? Why are you so calm? How are you so certain?" she asked, fisting his shirt in her hands.

"Because I was alone before. Now I have you. Even if I cannot believe in myself, I will always believe and have faith in you. Always."

Mya grasped the strands of Erik's hair as he kissed her, twirling them in her fists to try to keep him close to her. And he held her as if she were his whole world, the key to his entire being.

When they broke apart, she whispered, "I'm sorry for walking away from you, and for being so..." She looked down and mumbled, "difficult."

He grasped her chin, leaving her no way to retreat from him, and said with a smile on his face, "You are not difficult. You were scared and hurt. I understand that. I understand you, and I always will."

Erik rested his forehead against hers and for a moment they simply shared their breath.

"*Fagr skjaldmær min,* will you let me do this? I can't without you, not without your permission and your faith in me."

She gulped and held him tighter. "Promise me you'll come back."

"I promise. We have a lifetime to heal and live through together, and I refuse to waste a single moment of it."

She nodded and they kissed once more. He reached down and took one of her hands in his, and together they opened the door and returned to the rest of the group.

Mya looked at them, saw the empathy in their eyes, and it made her shy. "I'm—"

"Mya and I have discussed it. I am willing to bait the enemy so we can finish this war once and for all, but only if every possible protective measure has been taken."

Erik's tone was authoritative, and she straightened as some of her fear melted away.

"I'm sure you all know that I have been kept away from Mya for the last three hundred years. I'm not willing to spend another second without her. This plan must work. I will not move forward if there is even a slight probability of me not returning to her side at the end of this. Does anyone here have any objections to that?" Erik asked, then turned to her and smiled.

Mya nestled into his side, wrapping an arm his waist

as she watched her own family and friends smile and shake their heads.

"Then let us end this war once and for all."

———

There were several steps to their plan.

The first involved Oaklynn casting her own locator spell on Erik. To do so she needed to share her blood with him, and she shared a drop with everyone else who would be fighting alongside them as a precaution.

Oaklynn had also confirmed Mya's healing ability extended beyond physical ailments to abilities, spells, and curses that affected her mental or emotional states. Knowing Constance wouldn't give up the chance to try and take control of a single member of their group, Oaklynn and Astrid created an enhancement with Mya's blood that would temporarily act as a cure should any of them begin to fall under Constance's magic. It would only work once, so they had to act with caution. Since Astrid had created threads between them, they would be able to feel the mental slip in one of their comrades and get them to safety before they lost them all together.

Then they ran through different scenarios. Erik estimated that Constance had at least two hundred vampires when he'd last seen her at the cave, so for safety they doubled those numbers. Neither Johanna nor Erik remembered there being any older vampires, meaning they would be newly turned and weak. Daniella would use her ability to boil each vampire's blood, which, due to their connection to Constance, would at least weaken and distract her while Oaklynn would work to drain Constance's power and stop her from being able to cast stronger magic.

While it seemed things should go in their favor, Oaklynn warned they needed to keep as much of Constance's army alive as they could. If they outright killed them, Constance would be able to use their blood for more powerful and dangerous spells.

They each had their roles and weapons, so all that was left was for Oaklynn to cast a spell which would make Erik appear to still be under Constance's curse. He would then make his way to the old church to be kidnapped and delivered back to their enemy.

Mya hated it all. No matter how hard she tried, she couldn't let go of the fear that was eating away at her heart.

Erik placed his hand on her chest, right over the beating organ. "The day they took me away from you, you had a bad feeling. You warned me of it several times and I didn't listen to you when I should have. If you have that feeling right now, this all ends. I won't go and we'll find another way. Do you?"

She took a deep breath, but she already knew the answer. "No, I don't."

The corner of his lip tipped up in a half smile. "And

you told me Daniella's spirits tell her things. She hasn't warned us away from this, correct?"

Mya looked down. "No, she hasn't."

He tipped her head back up to meet his eyes. "You are my mate. You are my wife. I am going to build a home with you, in your house or somewhere else if you like, and I am going to fill that delicious cunt of yours with my come so often, that I'll keep your beautiful belly round with our children, no matter many you want. We'll have our home, our family, and all of this, all our pain and strife and the chaos we've gone through will fade away. This is the last part of that chapter of our lives, *fagr skjaldmœr min.* Trust me."

Erik cupped her cheek and she leaned into his hand, feeling his warmth. Mya parted her lips on a sigh when he bent down and kissed her, and she kissed him back with every part of her being.

"If you don't come back to me, I will find you and drag you back from the deepest pits of Tartarus only to kill you again myself."

He grinned proudly, squeezing her hand. "There's my queen." He kissed her once more and squeezed her hand. "It's time to go."

CHAPTER 20

Mya hated how seamlessly their plan worked. Constance's goons had taken Erik not long after he'd been spotted making his way back to the church.

She'd had to watch them kick and punch him, and sit by while they dragged him back to their car and drove away. Mya wanted to go after them, to wage war against them for even *daring* to lay one finger on him, but Greg had put a hand on her tightly balled fist and reminded her that this would all be over soon. No matter how much it killed her, she had to see this through.

She'd been silent the entire time they'd followed the car, caught between the fear that they would somehow lose him and the rationale that she had to believe in him, that they'd done everything to make sure he'd be safe. Mya, along with her family, Greg's seconds-in-command, Merida and Dominick, Lily, Oaklynn, Astrid, and the rest of the battle officers watched from the forest as Erik was led down an old mine shaft tunnel.

Then they saw the signal: Erik's fire flashing brightly outside of the entrance. Mya ran to meet him, and when she laid her eyes on him, she felt as though she could finally breathe again.

"Hi," she said softly, reaching out her hand to his.

Erik clasped her hand and smiled. "I missed you too, *fagr skjaldmær min.*"

"Have you run into anyone?" Greg asked.

"No, but I'm certain that explosion will bring someone our way," Erik said, before turning and walking with the group through the tunnel.

He was proven right two minutes later when a stampede of footsteps dashed toward them. Erik shot out his fire and incinerated them, leaving ash in their wake.

As they continued walking, Merida whispered, "I don't like this. It's too easy."

"Do you think she's testing us?" Dominick, her husband, asked.

"We just brought a bunch of strong immortals *to* her. It's what I would do," Merida said.

Greg nodded. "Everyone, stay on guard and keep your distance for as long as possible. Fight magic with magic until we know what we're dealing wi—"

"Stop!" Merida shouted. "Lily, check the walls."

Lily moved forward and held up a hand. The air vibrated for a moment as she used her power over metal, and then a crack sounded on either side of the wall before two angled metal sheets fell not even a foot in front of the group, their sharpness cutting through the air. If they had been standing under them, they would have been sliced in half.

Merida had been right. Constance either knew they were there or had been expecting them to find Erik. She'd prepared for them. The trap would have left them defenseless until their organs and limbs grew back, a process that would take weeks without necessary care. That meant Constance's aim was to capture, not kill.

They walked on slowly, methodically checking for traps and using their magic to kill the few groups of enemies that rushed toward them. But Mya knew it was all part of Constance's plan; their slow pace gave her time to fortify herself against them.

But there was only one outcome here, one destiny for that bitch, and it was to be impaled by one of their swords. That *would* happen. They would end this war today, and they would be *victorious*.

They finally entered the main area of the mine shaft, and as if summoned by her thoughts, Mya laid her eyes on the woman with long red hair, blue-green eyes, and an air that reeked of malice. Mya had to grind her teeth to stop herself from throwing a sword right at her head. She felt Erik's hand stroke the back of hers, tempering her fury, and she returned the action to comfort him as well.

Constance clapped her hands together and stood

from a makeshift throne. At her movement, hundreds of vampires flanked her sides. Mya's ears twitched as she heard more vampires waiting in the numerous tunnels that sprawled out from the main cave. By her estimate, they were up against almost five hundred vampires.

Constance's eyes scanned the group, and when they landed on Greg, she snarled. "You have killed so many of my family. You've attacked and raided my houses and tried at every chance to break apart my kingdom. You are a *traitor* to your own kind and unfit of being a ruler."

Greg shrugged, a smirk playing on his lips. "I would offer my condolences, but I truly don't give a shit."

Constance's eyes glowed red momentarily, but then she shook herself from her blood lust. She stood straighter, angled her head back, and glared at Greg. "Bow before me. Beg for my forgiveness and acknowledge me as your queen"—Constance licked her lips, her eyes glazing over with desire—"and I will let your family live here with me. We could be one. We could stop all these wars and let vampires rule the world as we were meant to. Our children would be safe."

Daniella's jaw ticked. "You say you are a queen"—she rotated her wrist, cracking it before taking out her sword and pointing it at Constance—"then as a queen, know that you will die tonight watching your kingdom burn to the ground."

Constance screeched, and they attacked.

Daniella unleashed her power, and it hit their enemies like a shockwave. The vampires in the cave staggered, as did Constance, but even Daniella couldn't take on five hundred at one time. In tandem, Johanna slipped into their minds to send them to sleep, but it was a trap. Every single vampire's head exploded, sending chunks of their brains through the air as their blood coated the walls and pooled on the floor.

Erik took over, using his power to navigate the tunnels and incinerate the bodies he found, but Constance's army just kept coming, and now he was the target.

"They're backing us into a corner," Mya growled.

"Fight. We'll clean up as we go," Greg said, and that was all she needed to hear to launch into action. Mya dashed from vampire to vampire, cutting off their heads with ease, but there were still too many of them. They needed to slow them down.

A loud crash echoed through the tunnel, and Mya turned back to see that Daniella and Johanna were using their abilities to block the entrances, sending rock and dirt tumbling onto their enemies. It wouldn't hold them forever, but it would help for now.

Then Mya heard the unmistakable click of a guns. Dozens of them.

"Get behind me, now!" Greg yelled.

The group formed behind him, and Greg pulled in

the darkness, molding it into matter that he used as a giant shield. But it wouldn't be enough to hold off the military grade weapons for long.

Daniella erected a large wall of earth, then fed her power of darkness into Greg's to make his shield stronger for the attack. She wavered but kept pouring in her power, and it was then Mya realized what was truly happening. Constance was trying to wear Daniella out. Without her, they would suffer a massive hit to both their offense and defense. The same would've happened if Johanna had gotten caught in the mental traps Constance had set.

The guns went off, and Mya made her way to Daniella. Her magic held for the first round, but the second round began to make it through, and Daniella groaned. She staggered to the side, but Mya caught her before she could hit the ground.

"Luke, feed Greg your shadows! They're trying to take Dani down!"

Luke shifted his focus, blending his shadows into the darkness to help reinforce Greg's shield against the attack while Mya cut at her wrist and held it to Daniella's mouth.

"Drink," she ordered.

Daniella bit down, and Mya rushed her healing power into her.

"Oaklynn, we need to kill them. We don't have any more time to waste!" Dom said.

"Dom's right!" Merida called from her husband's

side. "The vampires are starting to climb out of the rubble. We're going to be sitting ducks!"

"Then we'll have to end this fast. If Constance reclaims their blood, we're fucked," Oaklynn said.

Mya watched as Johanna nodded. The air grew humid around them, then she shouted, "Go now! I've frozen the vampires in place, so they won't be able to shoot!"

"Turn their guns on them! Kill everyone you can. I'm going after Constance," Greg said. He lowered the shield at the same time Lily turned the guns on the vampires and fired, shooting them in their heads. A bullet grazed Constance's arm before she ducked, and Greg dashed toward her.

The group worked their way through the hordes of vampires. Mya cut another one down, then paused and watched as his blood began to move as if it had a life of its own. Turning, she saw that the same thing was happening to all vampires she'd killed, their blood gathering, then traveling away from their bodies as if being drawn toward something.

"What the—"

"Stop!" Oaklynn screamed, causing Mya and Erik to look up at the large red shield Constance had erected. "You have to kill Constance, *now!* She's casting a reanimation spell!"

"What?" Erik shouted and blasted another array of fire at his targets before they rushed back to Oaklynn.

"Reanimation allows her to raise her fallen enemies'

bodies and control them. And with how many we've slain..." Oaklynn trailed off, her mouth open in horror.

"How do we kill them?" Mya asked, twirling her sword and decapitating another vampire.

"You won't be able to! We have to stop her, right now!" Oaklynn screamed.

But Mya and Erik couldn't stop killing the vampires. If they did, they'd be overrun. Mya looked around to see most of their group in the same predicament, while Greg fought to both defend himself from vampires and break through a shield of magic Constance erected.

"Take care of the vampires. I have to help Greg!" Daniella reached down to the ground, and her eyes glowed red as she pulled in more power from the earth. The boulders from the rubble lifted and she slammed them at Constance's shield, but to no avail.

"Astrid, Oaklynn, Dani, we need to link our powers!" Johanna yelled.

Astrid stood in the center of the four of women. The threads she'd woven between each member began to manifest and glow, sending purple sparks through the room before they dimmed to the four shared between them. Daniella and Johanna shared a knowing look before Daniella began to issue orders.

"Oaklynn, see if you can bind yourself into her blood magic so I can work through you. Astrid and Luke, try to find cracks in her shield. We just need one for Johanna to do what she needs to. Erik, you're the strongest of us. Try to smash that shield."

They tried. The tried with all their magic and abilities and might to break the shield, but nothing was working. Mya was growing increasingly frustrated, and when she gestured to the others that the dead vampires had begun to twitch, they knew they were running out of time.

In a last-ditch effort, Daniella used her power to break the ground beneath Constance. It buckled, and for one single moment, her concentration slipped and the shield cracked. Seeing the opening, Luke slipped his shadows inside and tied Constance's legs and arms, while wrapping a shadow around her neck.

Johanna used her power to break into Constance's mind, and froze her mouth mid-sentence, ending her chant. Then Greg struck at the shield again and finally, it fell away.

In one glorious last stroke, Erik lifted his sword and decapitated Constance, sending her head flying before it hit the ground with a hard *thump*.

The battle still raged on, but they were on the winning side now. They pushed back at Constance's minions, easily defeating them even in their large numbers, until they were the only ones left standing.

But instead of celebrating the end of their century long battle, Greg issued an order. "Split up and move out. I want this place searched top to bottom."

"What's wrong?" Mya asked.

"Something doesn't add up. Did it look like we just

fought a maniac to you?" Greg said, grabbing one of the guns off the ground and checking the chamber.

"No," Erik said, sliding his sword back in its sheath as he moved to stand beside Mya.

"Exactly. Constance planned for us, and she shouldn't have known we were coming. Erik killed everyone who appeared at your house. No one ever came to ours, so how did she know?" Greg asked.

Merida sheathed her weapons as she added, "And then there were our powers. I understand Dani's and Jo's from previous battles, but..."

Greg nodded. "She knew I wouldn't be able to hold off that many guns forever, and that's information not many outside of our battle officers know."

Greg grabbed Daniella's hand and the two led the group down one of the passageways.

"We need to find paperwork, clues, a computer, anything that can provide insight as to how Constance knew so much about us," Greg instructed.

As they walked, they disarmed traps and found several cages coated in the blood, skin, and organs of Constance's victims. Then they came across a metal door with a digital keyless lock. Mya moved to the front of the group and disarmed the lock, then Greg threw open the door. Once his gaze swept through the room, he signaled it was safe for them to enter.

They filed out into the room, each taking up a section to survey and comb through. Mya spotted a computer and sat down, using her hacking software to break into the system. Greg stood beside her and flipped through several pieces of paper he'd retrieved from a bookcase. "Shipping details, inventory, it's all here. They got this all in last night."

A loud crash called their attention, and they turned to see Daniella staring at the back of the picture that she'd pulled out of a frame. "Who is Katherine Martin?" she asked.

Greg and Lily moved toward Daniella, and she handed them the picture, pointing to the back.

"I don't know—"

Lily snatched the photo from him, flipping from the front to the back of the picture repeatedly. Then a look of shock came over her and she gasped. "Katherine Martin was Francois's daughter. He reported her missing three hundred years ago. The investigation was never closed."

Greg's eyes narrowed and he leveled his gaze at her. "Lily, the only people outside of my circle who knew we were coming here today was The Council."

She staggered back. "Greg, Francois is an ass, but he wouldn't go this far—"

"Actually, he would," Mya said, her voice shaking, and the group circled around her.

"I traced the routing number that's been funding Constance's operation. It goes through a lot of shell companies and offshore accounts, but I was able to hack into their system. The account is registered to The Diamond Group, of which Francois is the CEO."

Lily shook her head. "But that's not enough to prove that it's him. It could be anyone."

"Except he emailed Constance this list." Mya brought up the secure document and scrolled to the bottom slowly. It was a list of several hundred names, most of which were crossed off. At the bottom were theirs, along with their powers and weaknesses and all the other data they had been forced to share with The Council.

Erik's eyes grew wide. "Francois was the last person to be approved to join The Council. He's who we saw the day I disappeared."

It was Mya's turn to gasp. "But why? What would getting you out of the picture do?"

"It would give him control of The Council," Greg said. "I was going to be the leader. If anything happened to me then it would then go to Erik, and then the next strongest person, Francois. I think Francois knew you were Erik's mate, Mya. He knew if he pushed you hard enough you would kill the blood witches for him, and if you didn't then they'd kill us."

Lily nodded. "And with Greg giving up his seat to save your life, Francois would be free to lead The Council until Greg had concluded his investigation into Erik's supposed death."

"But with the wars…" Mya's eyes widened.

"Exactly. I've been too busy to investigate Erik's whereabouts, meaning Francois has been able to gain power and replace our seats as he sees fit," Greg said, slamming his fist onto the desk.

Mya turned to Erik and found his face and eyes brimming with anger. The man they trusted, the man their *people* had trusted, was a traitor responsible for centuries of their pain.

Greg dialed a number on his phone and put it to his ear. "This ends tonight."

CHAPTER 21

Francois was just on the other side of this door.

Erik could imagine Francois sitting down with a smile on his face, likely overjoyed that Erik and possibly several members of Mya's family—maybe even Mya herself—were dead. Erik wanted to rip the man apart.

Not only was Francois behind his capture, but Mya had found the incriminating information they needed to prove he was the one enslaving witches. Francois had been the original cause of the blood witches. He had supplied them with the immortals to target. He was behind the deaths of hundreds, the torture of thousands. Erik remembered the faces of the women Zachariah and Constance had stolen, raped, and brutalized, the men they'd forced to change into immortals and driven so mad that killing them was a mercy.

Francois was the reason why Greg had almost lost Daniella, why Johanna was still attending therapy for the scars he'd left on her psyche. He was why she had to be guarded and hidden from the public or else she'd be hunted down and captured again, why her family had to hide in the Fae Realm. But worst of all was that Francois was the reason for Mya's pain, for the healing they would need to work through together, for the days, years and centuries that had been stolen from them. They had no idea what other secrets he had hidden or who else he'd hurt since the time of being acting leader of The Council. But they would, *very* soon.

Finally, it was time for the meeting to begin. Greg, Erik, and Luke walked into the room, and Francois's face fell. Erik noticed that the faces of several other members did as well, while others averted their eyes in mock shame.

Francois wasn't working alone. There was more corruption here they still had to uncover, and from the way Greg's stance had changed, he'd noticed it too.

"Council, I come before you with incredible news. As you can see, Erik is alive." Greg's eyes narrowed as he stared right at Francois. "Much as I had expected."

Francois donned a mask of surprise as he stood. "My god," he gasped. "I can't believe it! Where have you been? Where did they find you, Erik? Why did you leave The Council?"

Erik's jaw ticked, but he swallowed back his anger and smiled. "I was captured by blood witches."

Several of The Council members gasped, then whispered to themselves.

"For all this time?" Francois asked.

"I thought they were all gone!" a member exclaimed.

"If they could capture him, they could capture us!" another member said, and several others murmured in agreement.

"They must be made our top priority!" Francois said.

Erik, Greg, and Luke all shared a look. Misdirection? The man was incredulous.

"I believe there are other matters that must be dealt with first," Greg said.

"Nothing is more important than the safety of vampires, *Gregori*," Francois hissed.

"I've had enough of this, shut up," Luke barked.

Francois drew back. "How dare you—"

Greg pushed a button and the projection screen behind them came to life.

"Oh, we dare," Greg said bitterly. "Just like you dared to be the mastermind behind this entire war, Francois!"

Greg opened the bundle of documents and they spread across the screen, displaying all of Francois's crimes. The man's eyes grew wide, his jaw falling open in horror.

Then he ran.

Francois reached the door and threw it open, only to come face to face with Mya. She grabbed him by his neck, hoisted him into the air and slammed him onto the ground. Then she buried her knee against his throat and growled, "You're not going anywhere."

The Council guards arrived a moment later and took Francois away. Erik and Mya shared a look of adoration and love before she slipped back out the door.

Greg smirked. "Now, I believe there are several orders of business we need to attend to."

———

The meeting ended with Erik and Greg reinstated as members of The Council, and Greg reclaiming the role of leader. Their next order of business was to find out everything Francois had done. They raided his office and sent battle officers to his home. Once they had their hands on every piece of evidence they could find, Erik, Greg, and Luke took Francois to a secret location and tortured him for hours.

It didn't take much to get him to reveal all the things he'd done and the people he'd worked with, including some of guards and council members, just as they suspected. Then Erik had gotten the pleasure of killing him, *slowly*.

The evening was both chaotic and cathartic. It had been a long time since Erik had gotten the opportunity to work with Greg and Luke, and at moments it brought him back to the past. He was proud of the men he'd spent so much of his life with. He was especially proud of who they'd become and how they'd gone on to grow without him, and he felt honored to be able to share a space in their lives once more.

They each changed into a new pair of clothes, and Erik burned their old ones along with Francois's body before they left and made their way to Greg's car.

"It's been a ... wild couple of days," Luke said, sliding into the back seat.

"It has been, but at least now everything is as it should be." Greg's eyes flickered to Erik's as he turned on the ignition. "Now, let's go home."

An idea formed in Erik's mind at Greg's words. "Can we stop off somewhere first? There's something I need to check."

———

Mya ran a hand through her long curly hair.

She'd kept herself busy while Erik was gone. She'd tidied the house, changed the sheets, did everything she could possibly think of to keep her mind busy until she'd passed by the room she'd made Erik's shrine for the fifth time. Then she blew out a harsh breath and decided it was time.

For years the shrine had been all she'd had left of him, but now she could touch him, hold him. If she wanted to start moving forward and building a life with Erik, she'd need to get rid of her old vice first.

She stared at his eyes in the picture, looked over his long blonde hair, his frame, and realized that although this portrait was exact in its likeness to him, it was missing his spark the liveliness in his eyes. It was something no one could capture, not even the greatest artist or sculptor. Erik was a masterpiece all on his own, and this replica and all the time she spent using it as a way to keep her connection to him was no longer needed.

Decided, she pulled it down from the wall with a large sigh and felt a weight lift off her shoulders. Then she stared at the empty spot. The portrait had been there for so long that the wall was discolored around it. Mya wiped away the dust, threw away the candles and decided to move the console to the entry way. She rested his picture there. Perhaps in time they would take others, make a family wall out of it. She smiled as the feeling of bliss settled within her.

A family, with him.

She'd wanted that for so long, and to know it was finally obtainable meant everything to her. That thought spiraled through her and led her to check the front door once more to see if Erik was back. A lance of fear sliced through her heart, and she wondered if that would ever go away, if she would ever stop worrying every time he was away from her.

Then she heard Greg's car door slam, and she smiled. Mya opened the front door, her grin growing as Erik took long, sure steps toward her. When he reached the threshold, she tilted her head up to his.

"Hello, love."

"Hello, *fagr skjaldmær min,*" he said, smiling back at

her. Then she was in the air, wrapping her legs around him while he kissed her and kicked the door closed behind them. He nuzzled her neck as he set her back down, then turned and looked at the changes she'd made.

"The real thing is much better to look at," she said breathlessly.

Erik cupped her cheek and she leaned into his touch, her eyes fluttering closed.

"Mya," he croaked, and her eyes flew open to meet his.

He paused, and she squeezed his arms. "Erik, what is it?"

"No, it's just..." He trailed off, and she tilted her head in confusion. He frowned before clearing his throat. "This is harder than I thought it would be."

"What is it? Just tell me what you need to say. I can take it, I swear," she said, even as a million horrible thoughts flashed through her mind.

Erik took her hands and kissed them. He seemed to relax at simply being able to touch her, and then he fell to one knee.

"Erik?" she gasped.

He slipped something out of his back pocket, and in between his fingers stood a white gold ring. Its prongs were shaped like leaves, and in each of them stood a green diamond. The metal twisted and turned like stems, all coming to surround another large green diamond at the center.

Her eyes widened. "Erik, is that...?"

He smiled. "Yes, I went back and I was able to find it." He swallowed. "Mya—"

"Yes!"

He stared at her in a mixture of shock and awe. "...what?"

She fell to her knees and wrapped her arms around him. "Yes! Yes!" she repeated, basking in his scent, his breath, the feel of his skin against her own.

Erik laughed, and each rumble shook her body. Tears of joy poured from her eyes. He kissed every inch of her skin, then they broke away just enough for her to watch as he slipped the ring onto her finger.

"You didn't even let me finish my proposal," he said, in mock sadness.

"I didn't need to. My answer was yes. It has always been yes, and it always will be."

Erik cupped her cheeks and kissed her like she was his everything, and she kissed him back just as intensely, just as passionately. His arms went around her waist while hers went around his neck, then he lifted her until she was pinned against the wall. Mya wrapped her legs around him and he pressed further into her. She could feel his erection hard and thick against her stomach, and she moaned, her hips tilting, core pulsing at the thought of having him inside her again.

"May I touch you?" he whispered against her lips.

"*Please*," she begged, pushing his blazer off his body and onto the floor.

"I'll be rough with you," he murmured as he trailed his lips over her skin. "I *have* to be rough with you."

"I can take it," she whispered. "I won't break."

He shifted, tilting his body from hers and sliding his thigh between her legs. His hands went to her ass and he squeezed her tightly, then he ground his thigh against her clit, and she moaned.

"Yes, you will, *fagr skjaldmær min*. You will take it. You will take everything I give you and you will beg for more. You will break for me." He licked her neck. "You always break so beautifully for me."

Her nipples grew so hard that every time they brushed against her shirt it was too much. Electricity and chills raced over each part of her body, setting her aflame. She was so sensitive for him, so turned on, so desperate to have all of him that she knew he was right; she would take him, would do whatever he wanted, would please him in whatever way he needed, as long as he made her come.

He hoisted her higher, forcing her to widen her legs and seat herself fully on his thigh. The pressure made her cry out, as his hand wound into her hair and tugged her head back against the wall. His eyes were so dilated, the irises nearly fully black, and when he inhaled, she knew he could smell her desire.

"Is that for me?" he growled.

"Yes," she whimpered, her hips grinding against him of their own accord, chasing her release.

"Good girl," he murmured against her temple, kissing the spot, and she moaned at his praise. "That's my good, precious girl. Always so happy to please me."

"Yes," she cried as he pushed against her harder. She squeezed his biceps and together they fell into a rhythm that was theirs, would forever be only theirs, and he took her higher and higher.

"I can feel it," he growled into her ear, tracing the lobe with his tongue, sending goosebumps all the way down to her toes. "I can feel how wet your pretty little cunt is for me."

She groaned, embarrassed at how true his words were and how they made her even wetter. Mya turned her head away from him even as she continued to grind against his thigh, the movement as necessary to her as breathing.

"I can *hear* it," he groaned. "It's like music to my ears. But you know what I want, *fagr skjaldmœr min*, so give it to me." He licked the pulse of her neck. "Give me your cries. Sing for me, my beautiful queen."

His teeth slipped into her neck, and she cried out in pleasure. She ripped at his shirt, needing to feel his skin, to press her nails into his back as she continued to buck against him. He moaned at the taste of her, at her noises, her cries, and then her head tilted back against the wall and she came for him. She broke apart for him, just as he had sworn she would.

Mya clung to Erik through her orgasm, but he kept drinking from her, kept pressing against her, and soon he began to work her to another one. He kissed her, the taste of her blood still on his lips as he bit, licked, and sucked her mouth. She slid her hands down to his belt and managed to undo the clasp before he ripped it out of the loops and wrapped it around her wrists. Then he tore at her clothes, ripping them until they were nothing but shreds that fell to the floor.

He pinned her hands above her head and tied the belt around her wrists, his eyes roaming over her body.

"Erik?" she panted.

"I'm well aware that you can get out of this. Don't, and I won't punish you." He said, then he lifted her, sliding her body up the wall while he trailed hot kisses over her skin. He licked and nibbled her collarbone, slid down to her breasts and sucked at one while he toyed with the other.

She arched her back, offering every inch of herself to him, and he smiled, sucking her harder. Mya wrapped her bound hands in his hair, holding his head to her chest as his hand slid over her stomach and down. After coating a finger in her wetness, Erik began to rub her clit in circles that had her undulating against him, her body begging for his touch, begging for him to use her however he wanted.

He pulled away from her nipple and slid his hand

down to her thighs. He spread her open, then lifted her legs over his shoulders. She gasped. She was five-foot seven-inches tall, and Erik was a foot taller than her. At this height, she could touch the ceiling.

"Erik?" she said, her voice husky and breathless.

He stared up to her, his head between her thighs, face so close to her pussy that every breath he exhaled gave her chills. "I've wanted to taste this for so long. I've dreamed about it."

She blushed. "Erik, you don't—"

He smacked her clit, and the sudden flash of pain and pleasure making her whimper and buck against his hand for more. "You won't deny me this, Mya. I need it, just like I need you. I need to know what you like, how you like it, how you taste, how you move when I kiss you here"—he ran his thumb over her clit—"or here"— he slid his thumb down, spreading her pussy lips—"or even here," he said, sliding his thumb over her asshole and making her breath hitch and her eyes widen. "I need to know every piece of you, and by the end of tonight there won't be a place I haven't touched, licked, or sucked."

Then he spread her folds, and she watched helplessly as he licked her pussy. The cry that left her lips was loud, and she was dripping with unabashed need, but it was the pleasure on his face that did her in, the way he closed his eyes and moaned at the taste of her.

"My own ambrosia, the sweetest nectar of the gods."

"Erik," she moaned his name as he gave her a long, deep, slow lick, making her body quiver.

"You are my goddess, Mya. I prayed for you. I pray to you, and now I will worship you until we are both sated." His eyes burned bright, silver glowing with red. "Don't deny me, my goddess. Show me what you like, and when I get it right, reward me with your cream."

He ate her. He devoured her. He sucked, and nibbled, and licked her in every way possible until her back arched, her hips bucked, and she rode his tongue while her thighs shook. She came all over his face, and then he did it again, and again, and again. He sucked her clit until her eyes rolled back into her head. Then he slapped her pussy, slid three fingers inside of her, and curled them to reach a spot that had her screaming his name once more.

He bit her thigh while he pumped his fingers, rubbing her clit with his thumb until she felt an odd sensation, something new. She both chased it and ran away from it, grabbing Erik's hair and tugging him against her one moment, then trying to push him away the next. Before she could stop herself, she came so hard she squirted all over his hand.

His eyes glazed over with lust as he cleaned her with his tongue, then drew some of the wetness down to her asshole. It shouldn't have felt good for him to rub her there, for his thumb to slide over the rim of her hole, but it did, by the gods it did. It felt so good that she came again from his touch, from the way he sucked her clit, from the way he worked against her asshole. When his hand wrapped around her throat, she screamed his name and saw stars.

He pulled her back from the wall, lowering her slowly until she was on the floor. "Hold onto me," he ordered, and she did, half delirious as he broke open the closure of his pants.

His cock sprang free and she moaned at the sight of it, so swollen, red, and dripping pre-cum all for her. Erik squeezed the back of her leg, throwing it over his forearm. The position caused her hips to tilt to the side as he continued to spread her, then he pressed his cock to her pussy and rammed all the way to the base.

She screamed out, her voice growing higher in pitch as he slammed into her. He was brutal with her, possessive, grasping her neck and forcing her to watch him, to stare into his eyes as he undid her with his every stroke. He was in her, around her, taking her, claiming her, fucking her with wild abandon, but when they came together it felt like nothing else. Her pussy clamped down on him, begging for every single drop of come in his balls, and he gave it all to her.

When Erik pulled out of her, she thought they were done, but then he spun her around, pulled her ass back and ground against her. "This hungry little cunt is going to take me again," he whispered into her ear.

"Erik," she groaned, her nipples rubbing against the wall with his every move. "It's too much, I can't … I *can't.*"

He smacked her ass, angled her hips, and thrust in so deep she cried out.

"You can." *Thrust.* "You will." *Thrust.* "You want this." *Thrust.* "You want me," he growled.

She screamed his name as he spanked her ass over and over, then she pushed back against him, spreading her legs, wanting to feel him deeper inside her, wanting to take him harder.

"Beg for it," he groaned, nails pressing into her ass cheeks as he pulled her back.

Tears of pleasure poured from her eyes as she turned her head to his. "Please!"

"Please, *what?*" he commanded, fucking her harder, pushing her closer to the edge.

"More. I need more. Harder. Deeper. I need … I need you, don't stop, don't stop, *don't stop!*"

"Good girl," Erik purred, then he bit her neck, and she came. Liquid rolled over her thighs but she didn't care, too lost in her orgasm and the way he continued to fuck her. She ripped the belt apart, her hand grabbing his hair to hold him against her as he continued to use her pussy, to pound into her with utter abandon.

They came once more. Then he took her on the floor. He made her ride him on the couch, bent her over the chair, then ate her as if she was his favorite meal on the dining room table, before he took her again. They washed each other in the shower, and Erik ate her once more. He drew her a bath to ease her body, but she had moved past the point of no return, and when he neared the bathtub, she took his cock into her mouth and sucked him until he came, swallowing it all.

They relaxed for an hour together in one another's arms, until he moved them to the bed, where he gently took her again and again. She slept for hours afterward, naked and basking in the warmth of his body until mid-afternoon, when he brought her breakfast and made her come once more.

Every word, every caress, every time he slid inside her was a reclaiming of her heart and her soul, and she would stay by his side until the day time stood still.

EPILOGUE

The corruption they'd uncovered implicated six other members of The Council. Erik and Mya were part of the teams that hunted down the perpetrators, tortured them, and uncovered their secrets.

They did their best to find those that had been harmed and get them justice, but Erik also had to fill his seat on The Council. At Greg's, Dani's, Johanna's and Mya's urging, Luke finally agreed to take one of the open seats. Merida took another, and they eventually filled the remaining seats with good, dedicated people who wanted a better world for vampires and all immortals.

The answer was to create The Agency, a place where anyone, even humans, who had suffered at the hands of an immortal could go for help. The Agency was the answer against war, against the darkness and tragedy they had suffered. It was how they planned to create a better world for their future generations.

Generations like Mya and Erik's double set of twins, and the baby currently kicking in her stomach. It had taken years of therapy and vulnerability to get to this point, and even then, Erik sometimes found himself absorbed in the bleakness of his world, reliving all those years without Mya.

But they were happy, and when he looked at her, when he felt their unborn child kicking in her stomach, when he saw the wedding band on her finger, the wall of photos of their family, when he heard the laughter of their children, even their fighting and tantrums, it all made sense. It was all worth it. And if he had to, he would do it all again, go through every moment of suffering, just to get to this brilliant, beautiful space with her.

His wife.

His queen.

His goddess.

The mother of his children.

The other half of his soul.

Fagr skjaldmœr min.

The End of book 3, Night Fall: Chronicles of The Otherworld.

———

Want to read about a mafia queen who doesn't need anyone and the mafia king who will kill to stand by her side? Scan the QR code below!

Don't forget to join my newsletter to get a bonus scene of Mya's song, all the latest updates, ARC opportunities, and more!

ABOUT THE AUTHOR

Melissa had a difficult time speaking as a child, and thus writing became her best friend. There she learned the power of emotion, how to communicate heartbreak, sadness, tragedy, and still hope for something better: the happy ever after.

She loves to write imperfect, possessive heroes, that will risk their lives for those they love, strong heroines that can hold their own, and steamy scenes that grab you by the throat and bring you to your knees.

Melissa lives in a small town off the coast of Egypt, and is a huge mythology buff, with a love of all things magical, supernatural, paranormal, and steeped in lore and fantasy. When she is not writing Melissa can be found singing and dancing her heart out, or up, late at night, contemplating space and the universe with a large cup of tea.

facebook.com/MelissaCumminsAuthor

instagram.com/melissacumminsauthor

bookbub.com/profile/melissa-cummins

ACKNOWLEDGMENTS

To my editor, Ellen, thank you so much for all you've done.

Taylor, your feedback made me laugh out loud. Thank you for spending your time and energy on my characters and their story.

To you. Yes! You! Thank you so much for reading my novel. Knowing that you took the the time to read it is beyond amazing to me. You help every author to move forward, to write their next book, to publish, to celebrate. That's all you. So thank you again, take care, and I can't wait for you to read my next book!